THE GARDENS

OF

PRYME

AO356-12-54992

CHAPTER ONE

The tunnel disappeared into the blue distance until it came to a single point, a singularity, and no matter how fast the bubble travelled, the end of the tunnel came no nearer. The walls of the tunnel blurred past so quickly that the bubble appeared to be stationary, a bubble suspended inside an endless tube, suspended in time and space, apparently timeless, and it was only when another bubble travelling the other way flashed past, a brief burst of dazzling white light, was there any sense of movement. There was an occasional momentary visual hiatus when a junction appeared, no doubt also leading to another featureless, non-ending journey, and at times the bubble passed a service area, where drones appeared frozen in mid-task and then gone before the eye hardly had time to register their image on the retina. Nor was there any sound or vibration that would have indicated propulsion and motors. Presumably, the solid dark grey floor held the secrets to the bubble's function, but hardly large enough to house any propulsion unit.

The sole passenger of the bubble sat in a padded seat, as featureless as the bubble and tunnel, apart from the wings of the headrest that housed the communications. During almost the complete journey, pictures and messages were displayed on the interior of the helmet visor. He had passed the time by talking to friends and colleagues, passing and receiving messages, perusing items of news, and if totally desperate for distraction, a play or a film.

It was not often that someone travelled by bubble, there was usually no need; all could be accomplished from the comfort of one's home on viscom, and anything such as travelling physically would be usually undertaken by a drone. No doubt most of the passing bubbles had contained drones.

Stef Barak was tired and switched off the communicator with a short command and contemplated the reason for this journey. There was a report of an irregularity, and he was to make a physical check on Section AO356-12-54992, and report back to the City Council, and that request was unusual in itself. Irregularities were usually handled by the council directly, and in a few cases with the aid of drones, but Stef could not remember any investigating officer ever being sent to a location before this.

When as an adolescent, he would have used the bubbles as a game, but soon became tired of the infantile pursuit, as without a valid pass, he and his friends could not leave the tunnel except at the for Ellie.

THE GARDENS
OF
PRYME

AO356-12-54992

Mike Williamson

DEDICATION

To PJ,
The person who opened minds.

Books by this author
Science Fiction
THE DANCING LIGHTS
THE GARDENS OF PRYME
THE CENTAURI SCROLLS
THE CENTAURI SCROLLS II
THE GENESIS BUG. Awarded Publisher's Desk Gold Star
APOLLO'S FURY
THE OLD MAN AND THE STARS
Supernatural
DEERE HOUSE
OLD HOUSE. Awarded Publisher's Desk Gold Star
THE CAUSEWAY

We'll go more a'roving
By the light of the Moon.

Lord Byron

embarkation point. That was an almost forgotten period, and the memory passed as fleetingly as the walls of the tunnel. Ever since then, he and his friends had become more distant, separated by the walls of the vast complex of apartments that made up the City. Sure, they kept up their friendship, but the days of laughing as they physically tried to fill one of the bubbles with their bodies was just a distant fragment, almost someone else's life. As he thought of those times he drifted into a light sleep, and once more in his mind, the class of '08 were playing pranks on each other, their wild laughter ringing out against the solid, cold, featureless walls of the tenements.

He awoke when he felt an almost imperceptible deceleration. With a start, he realised that he had dozed off for most of the journey, something that he rarely had done, but he had never been on a journey of this magnitude. The walls now had features, the joint-lines of their construction flicking past, and they slowed down to stop at his disembarkation point. No signs to reveal the location, but the communicator confirmed that they had arrived before it lifted from Stef's head. There were no crowds of people jostling to board as he had seen on some old films; there were just two solitary drones that completely ignored him as they performed their tasks. He glanced at the drones, identical in every way but presumably they could tell each other apart.

There were no directions, just a single door that made it obvious that this was the direction to go. The transparency of the bubble vanished, and he stepped on to the platform, and as he stepped away from the bubble, it too vanished! He blinked and wondered if he

3

had been riding the tunnel at all! Without its human occupant, it had attained massive acceleration from a standing start and zoomed off to its next destination. If he still been in the bubble, he would have been crushed into a small package. It had never happened, as far as he knew, but it was a sobering thought.

The single door melted away as he approached it, revealing a moving pavement. It did not move until he stepped on to its slightly sticky surface, and without a jerk, it accelerated up to a speed that he could have easily attained while running. Now the air ruffled his shoulder length blonde hair, making him feel naked and exposed. He was not used to the winds of the upper surface, and as far as he knew, nor had anyone else that are alive today. The moving pavement came to a junction with three avenues in which to travel. It automatically chose the right-hand one without any indication as to where the break in the pavement occurred; it was as if all three were the same surface even if they went to different destinations. Now the pavement climbed effortlessly at the same speed, and all the time the same silence as on the road. He had absolute confidence that he would arrive at his destination, although there were still no signs to inform him where he was.

The pavement slowed, and a section of wall melted away. The pavement stopped precisely at this point, and he stepped through the doorway which filled again behind him as though there had never been a door there at all. Now he could perceive a faint hum, a tiny vibration of air molecules as the replaced the stale air.

The passage led to a large room, in which stood a woman waiting patiently for her guest.

What struck Stef as he stepped into the room were the large windows, three of them that showed a large garden full of colour and movement. It was an attractive scene, but not that unusual to him; he often changed one of the walls of his apartment into a fanciful scene, depending on his mood, but never three, or as large! That was unusual! A brief feeling of vertigo passed over him.

He quickly shifted his attention to the woman; she was the same height as he, and of indeterminate years; still young enough to be very attractive, but also old enough to have experienced life. Her one startling feature was a bronze skin, compared to Stef's pale complexion, framed by a wild shock of dark hair that cascaded over her shoulders. Her grey eyes had followed his gaze to the windows, and then to herself, and they now crinkled as she smiled a welcome.

"You must be Stef!" she said, although he could not have been anyone else! She thrust out her hand to take his. This startled and confused him; it was so long ago that he had reason to practice this form of greeting. Jerkily he pushed his hand forward and took her cool slim hand. It was then that he realised that she was not wearing the usual coverall; she wore some loose, white robe that exposed her brown arms and shoulders. Keeping a grip on his hand, she led him towards a luxurious sofa.

"I am Pryme. Please sit down, and I'll order some refreshment," she said, "Have you had a good journey?"

Stef blinked! What a strange question! Of course he had a good journey, he was here, wasn't he? "Y-yes." He stammered.

"Do you like my garden? I noticed that you were attracted to it," she smiled and turned towards the nearest window, "Perhaps later we can take a stroll through it."

Stef looked surprised, almost horrified! The thought of walking into a picture was unheard of! It had been explained to everyone in the class of '08 that the energy fields that created the picture would severely damage human tissue. There were even horror stories about people who ignored the advice!

Then his thoughts changed as a drone entered the room, carrying a tray of some delicate glasses and a carafe of amber liquid, and a plate of bite-sized food. The drone placed this on the low table before them. Drones do not enter a human's rooms – ever!

His face must have shown his surprise, for Pryme smiled, "That is Ega, my personal drone. I know that it is unusual to give drones a name, but she is so helpful, that I could not do without her. Please help yourself to the refreshments." Ega drifted quietly back from where she came, a room out of sight, and Stef jerked as he took in Pryme's statement.

"That is a waste of a drone!" he said firmly, "It could be better utilised elsewhere."

"I suppose that you just summon your needs and everything appears, just like everyone else has done for aeons," she was almost laughing at him, "Don't you want to feel another being next to you?"

6

"But a drone!" he waved vaguely at the direction the drone had taken. Never in his wildest dreams would he have considered a drone as a being!

"What is wrong with a drone?" Pryme's smile had vanished, and her face now took on the expression that matched the question.

"N-nothing, in its proper place!" he stuttered. He could not think of a reason other than it was never done.

"Feel the table," Pryme instructed, and Stef ran his fingers over the highly polished surface.

"Very nice," he said, "It is a good reproduction."

"It is not a reproduction; it is real wood!" Pryme said, her face appeared to be holding back a torrent of words and a flood of emotions.

"Of course it's wood!" Stef said, "You can order up any texture that you want!"

Pryme leant forward, revealing slightly more of her suntanned body than he expected, "No, it is real wood, from out there!" she pointed towards the windows and the waving plants with a long brown finger.

Stef drew back from the table, wiping the hand that had touched the offensive surface on his coverall. "It is full of disease!" he muttered.

"No, it's not!" Pryme replied, "That is the real world out there, and everything there has a beauty that we have ignored for far too long!"

"You can grow tables?" Stef edged further away from the table, as though it would spring up and attack him.

A peal of laughter rang through the room. "No silly! You take the raw material and fashion it into the shape that you want." Pryme was shaking with laughter.

"You can do this?" Stef was mesmerised by the table.

"Uh-uh, no! I tried, but the skills that we once had have atrophied." Pryme looked sadly at the table, "Ega made that, and the sofa that you are sitting on, the glasses, pottery, even the drink and pastries. She is quite clever!"

"But a drone isn't taught how to do such things!" Stef exclaimed.

"How do you know?" Pryme looked slyly at him.

"I, I ah," Stef sought for an answer, but again found none.

"Someone told you," Pryme answered her own question, "No one has actually shown you the proof, until now!"

Stef looked decidedly uncomfortable but said nothing.

"Do drones lie?" Pryme suddenly asked.

"I can't see why they should." Stef was starting to sweat, and the coverall should have prevented that. Things were going out of shape! He had been subjected to too many new experiences, confusing experiences that had caught him off guard.

Ega had quietly entered the room, as though summoned, or had she been listening, and stood patiently before them. Its slightly shiny surface reflected the green light from the Outside.

"Ega, please will you answer this man's questions as truthfully as possible," Pryme instructed the machine.

There was a slight movement as Ega focused on Stef. "I will do so!" The voice was not as tinny as Stef had expected, in fact, it was quite pleasant, then Ega did something that truly shocked him, she asked a question! "Are you Officer Stef Barak from Section Fourteen?"

Stef gaped open mouthed at the machine, as though it had grown another head, and he just managed to nod.

"I have often wondered about the other sections," Ega said, "Are they the same as here?" This was unheard of! A drone asking questions! It was impossible! In fact, Stef could not remember a drone ever talking! And a curious one to boot!

Recovering from the shock. Stef managed a reply, but in a dry, rasping voice, "Yes, more or less."

"Ask her some questions, or she'll never stop asking hers!" Pryme said.

Stef coughed to clear his by now parched throat, "Did you make this table?"

Ega bent and looked at the table, "Yes! Is there something wrong with it?"

"Who told you that you could make a table?" Stef ignored her question. Of course there was something wrong with it, it was made by a drone!

Ega struck an almost human pose as one who is recalling something, "I've always known how to make things. Don't you?"

"Who asked you to make this table, or these glasses and plates?" Stef asked, ignoring the drone's question.

"No one! Was it wrong?" Ega actually sounded worried.

Pryme intervened, "No Ega, Stef was just curious. You did well. Thank you!"

Ega turned and glided out of sight. Pryme turned towards Stef, "I didn't want you upsetting her. I don't understand how this happened, but I prefer her to continue to do what she does as it amuses her and myself."

Stef shook his head, "You call it by a name, and you have given it a gender, and you have allowed it to make all of these things, you are even concerned about its feelings. I think that is something peculiar, something beyond the normal!"

Pryme shook her head, and the brunette hair moved over her face and shoulders. "I did not do anything until she produced this table. She even persuaded me to wear this dress, which she also made. If this was made by a human, would you think that it was repulsive?"

Stef did not answer for a moment. The motion of her hair over her bare brown skin was strongly erotic, and when she moved the dress revealed parts of her body that was not the custom outside of mating, altogether too much!

He stood up. "I don't know what to think! I will have to return home and research on the question."

Pryme stood with him, her hand on his shoulder, her grey eyes looking directly into his. "Before you go, you should see the garden."

"I can see it, thank you!" Stef looked wildly at the windows. The feeling of vertigo returned.

"You must see it closer," Pryme's hand slid slowly down his arm, almost caressing it until she took his hand and gently guided him towards a window that had opened, vanished without his noticing. Stef was mesmerised by this strange but beautiful woman and felt that he would have followed her anywhere. As they stepped out into the garden, Stef's flinched, expecting some pain, instead his nostrils filled with a strange aroma, something new, something old and wet, something sweet and intoxicating.

Pryme noticed his flared nostrils, "That is the smell of life, growth, and of death," she said, "All life passes through the garden, from birth to death, and even beyond."

Stef shivered, not from her words, but from the cold feeling on his skin, little drops of moisture was falling on everything, including them! He looked upwards to find the source of the water, but all he could see were the round, convoluted bases of clouds. He had never seen clouds before, except in old movies.

"It's raining!" he cried in wonder. He had seen this on old films, but the City had no need for rain, as there were no plants or even humans in the grey streets for that matter. No, that was not totally true, he remembered his friends in the class of '08 running through the echoing, empty corridors of yesteryear.

"It will do you no harm," Pryme told him, "This is what provides the plants with life." She tugged him further into the garden, towards a group of towering silver trees.

"We can shelter here if it troubles you. This is my favourite spot," she said, "When it stops raining, and the sun appears, it is the most perfect place to be." Stef gaped up at the towering birch trees.

"They grow here?" He whispered. Then he frowned. From nearby he could hear something, an almost annoying tiny vibration.

"That is a bee," Pryme pointed at a flower, "It collects pollen, and takes it to a nest where it makes honey."

11

"You haven't given this a name, have you?" Stef bent down to look closely at the tiny insect almost buried in the flower head. He had never seen anything so small, or so active.

"I'm sure that it has a name, but only one that it knows, or its companions." As she spoke, Stef then noticed that other similar creatures were buzzing in other flower-heads. Pryme was watching him closely, anxiously waiting for a verdict. "I wanted to show you this above all else." She pulled him beyond the stand of trees. They were walking on a soft green carpet, small plants that he recalled were called grass.

Stef's jaw hit a lower level than ever before. Beyond the trees, the ground sloped down, covered in plants and more trees, and in the distance he could make out the shoreline of a vast expanse of water. That was enough to amaze anyone of Stef's background, but what shook him was the sight of two drones that were working diligently on something on the ground. Drones do not work in the Outside! There was no reason to do so!

He looked slowly round, taking in every detail until he faced the direction from where they came from. It was a strange sight; the window they stepped through was still open, and he could see into the room through all windows. Above that was a red cover, something he recalled was called a roof, and beyond that, soaring into the distant sky was a mountain. He had seen these before in the films, but to experience the sight, here in the open with the rain softly falling, was something else again! The mountain consisted of rounded bumps, one on top of the other, and then he realised that the mountain was what covered the City, it was the City! Now he could see that the green grass and trees were growing over the material of the City. Only Pryme's apartment revealed the existence of what lay beneath the turf.

"You live on the Outside!" he exclaimed, "How is that possible?"

Pryme shrugged, her garment slipping open to reveal even more of her brown skin. "At first I thought that the pictures were just that, a picture. Then Ega showed me that it was real. You have no idea what it is like some days and even the nights; it grows dark here, and the moon and stars gleam down. It is magical!"

"It grows dark, and you can see the stars?" Stef looked up again, and Pryme nodded, her hand still clutching his. Stef had never experienced true darkness, and the stars were a half-forgotten myth, stories told in kindergartens.

"This is a good day, sometimes it can storm, the winds blow, and the rain comes down in torrents. There is even the occasional thunder and lightning. It is purely magical," she repeated.

Stef nodded slowly, "And dangerous and frightening!" He had no idea what thunder and lightning were, but the words suggested some unknown power from ancient days, and something to be avoided.

Pryme pointed, "Those two drones and others look after the garden. They do not speak to me, and Ega says that she does not know them, but recently I found a bunch of flowers waiting for when the window opened. I wonder who laid them down!"

"This is too much to take in one go," Stef said, his mind was reeling. Never had he been exposed to the Outside, and it was a greater emotional experience than the old films had suggested. "I'll have to research what is happening. May I return at some later date, probably to take some readings?"

Pryme moved very close to him, and he became aware of her body scent that was so much like the garden, of wild flowers and herbs. "Of course you can come here! You're always welcome!" she said and looked deep into his eyes. Stef felt his pulse rate increase, and who could blame him; here he was standing next to a very attractive, half naked woman, in a place of wonder and magic. Yes, that was it, really magical, and in his mind, she was the most magical of all!

CHAPTER TWO

All the way home, he thought of the encounter. There was something almost primeval about Pryme, she was almost like one of the wild plants in her garden, or was it her garden? It was as though she was made from the garden, a part of it, and she belonged to the garden, to the wild reaches of trees, lakes and sky. He turned off the communications in the bubble, and let his mind run over the meeting. Before he left, he allowed himself to be persuaded to taste the drink and eat one of the cakes. They were pleasant, slightly fruity, and he guessed that they were also from the garden. He had never eaten or drank from nature before, and he found that it was strangely erotic, or was that flip of his stomach indigestion!

He arrived back in Section Fourteen, and as he stepped out of the bubble, his mind was far away as he made his way to his apartment. There was no one else on the streets and pathways, as usual. No windows opening on to the bustle of humanity that once filled the streets. His mind was so full of his experience that he had not noticed the long passage of time or the passing of the endless tunnel. He was fascinated by the old movies and considered himself something of an expert on the subject, and what he had seen today struck him as something from one of those movies. He entered his apartment, one of many in a featureless grey block, and ordered an armchair and a drink. Both materialised the drink on a small side table.

He threw himself into the chair and picked up the drink, and before sipping, he studied the glass and contents; it did not appear any different to the ones in Pryme's apartment. He sipped and immediately noticed a difference, it was somehow dead, while Pryme's drinks were full of life. He replaced the glass, and stroked the wood of the table; it felt the same, but he knew that this did not exist before he entered the apartment, and it would disappear when he was finished with it. He frowned, there was something uncomfortable with that arrangement. He could imagine Pryme returning home with everything waiting for her, somehow wanted. He looked around the sparse walls, comparing it with Pryme's pastel colours, little ornaments on her table, a vase with flowers from the garden. Had the drone made those as well?

Dismissing all thoughts of Pryme, he turned his attention to her apartment. One section of the wall became a screen on his command, and he searched the record for the address and having found it, discovered that it should have been exactly like his, with no possible contact with the outer surface. He was positive that Pryme was not capable of altering the apartment, the project was beyond the scope of anyone that he knew, so that left the drones, and they would not do so without specific instructions. As far as he could see, no alterations had been approved by the City.

He frowned. This was not just an irregularity; Pryme lived a life far different from anyone else than he had heard of, she dressed differently, she had drones acting as servants, and she had unrestricted access to the upper surface but was it illegal? The problem had become to one of how all of these changes occurred without anyone's authority. That must be the irregularity that he was sent to examine.

However much he scoured the records, as far back as the records went, he could find no mention of even planned alterations, so he turned his attention towards the drones. Can they be trained to make furniture, glass, pottery, and cook? To his surprise, he found that their basic training allowed for any future tasks and that they had a full knowledge of the basic elements for advanced and alternative education. He then tried to find any drones that had been specifically allotted to Pryme, or anyone else for that matter, and that led to a dead end.

Then his thoughts returned to Pryme, and he saw her as when he left her, the shimmering, flowing garment revealing all too much of her brown body. He shook his head to remove the tantalising vision, and returned to the records. From what he could see, she had been living in that apartment for close on seven terms, but there was nothing about her before that; no other accommodation. This must be a mistake! According to the official record, she was born, went to a school unfamiliar to him, but after that a blank. She had done next to nothing after her education.

After pondering on this conundrum for some while, he sighed and ordered a meal, plus a dining table. When they materialised, he blinked. Usually, when he ordered a meal, it was on a table suitable for one, and with a single chair, or on very rare occasions, two at the most, but this time it was a long table with intricate carvings and the two chairs similarly decorated. The table was set for two on a white Damask tablecloth, and between the two plates, both full of steaming food, stood two silver candle holders, the flames guttering as in a slight draft, although there was none in the apartment. As he stood and walked forward to examine this abnormality, a carafe of red wine appeared with two full glasses.

Stef picked up one of the silver knives, and then the other. They were definitely real, and his attention turned from them to the table; he had not ordered wine, and although he had not specified, the apartment's memory should have supplied a single meal, and he would not have ordered candles!

"Please remove the meals and table," he ordered, and everything blinked out of sight. "Now please provide a single normal meal for one person," and the normal single plain table and chair appeared with a single plate of food, and there were no candlesticks or silver cutlery.

He sat down and fiddled with the food, his mind wondering why the extravagant and unordered meal had appeared. Was there something wrong with the City Control? If there was, it could explain Pryme and her apartment.

The meal was then rapidly consumed, Stef having made up his mind to first check on City Control, before taking any steps to rectify the twin problems of Pryme and her apartment. No, a triple problem that included the drones. Now that he had a plan, he could sleep easily. A shower appeared in place of the table; he took off his coverall, throwing it carelessly to one side, but before it hit the floor it vanished.

The water cascaded over his head, warming and soothing, totally different to the cold rain that he experienced in Pryme's garden, and then a sudden thought spoilt the moment: if Pryme and her apartment should not exist, how could they rectify the problem? Whatever the records revealed, she did exist, so what could they do with her?

CHAPTER THREE

In the morning he moodily ate his porridge breakfast, wondering what Pryme would be eating; probably something from the garden, and he shuddered at the thought. He had once viewed a movie that showed minute creatures that commonly lived with humans in the past, and he thought that it was disgusting. What he was pondering on was Pryme's state of mind. He had heard some terrifying tales of the treatment of people who had become abnormal, erratic in their behaviour. The result was usually that the patient died or became totally mindless, and that led to euthanasia, the same result! Somehow he could not imagine that Pryme deserved such a fate.

He made contact with an old school chum, Elo, who did something technical in the City Control. An image appeared of Elo, but not just an image, a very realistic holographic image at the end of the room. It displayed Elo's room as a visual extension of both rooms. He was still eating his breakfast, and looked up with surprise at Stef's image that had appeared in his apartment.

"You get up early!" Elo exclaimed through a mouthful of porridge.

"Sorry! Is it too early for you?" Stef smiled, not even considering not to tease his old friend, "I hear that you people at City Control have a cushy number!"

"Hmm, I hear the same about you investigators!" Elo wiped his mouth on a napkin, and it and the table disappeared when he threw the napkin on the dish. "What can I do for you?"

Stef did not know where to start. He did not want to say too much; all of a sudden he became protective of Pryme and her lifestyle. "Has there been any unusual events with City Control?" he asked.

"What do you mean?" Elo frowned, "Everything is as normal, you know that City Control is self-rectifying. What sort of abnormality are you talking about?"

"I don't really know," Stef now wished that he had not made contact, "I was just wondering if anything unusual had happened, slight errors, that sort of thing."

Elo snorted, "There has never been an error with City Control in recorded history! I can assure you that nothing untoward has or can happen!"

Stef almost bit his tongue in preventing his blurting out that City Control makes all of the records, but it also gave him a direct question, "Has City Control ever made a wrong recording, failed to record something?"

Elo slowly shook his head, and in a sad voice replied, "I don't know where you're going with this, but City Control is faultless. Are you feeling well? You look a little flushed to me, and if I were you I'd call the medrone, you could be suffering from something." He was referring to the medical drone that was used for all medical functions.

"I'm feeling fine, but has anyone ordered something, and something different had appeared, such as the wrong meal?" Stef released a small part of the problem.

Elo laughed, "I should hardly think so! That is one of the fundamental functions and cannot go wrong. It would show up in other areas before that happened."

Stef thought that maybe other things had happened that Elo obviously did not know about.

"I think that you need some exercise," Elo said, "We have not seen you on the courts for a while, so give me a call next week, and I'll put some sparkle back into you!"

It was true; Stef had drifted away from his school friends more than the others, "Right then, I'll call you and see who has lost their sparkle!" He replied, also thinking that he might get some more information without obviously asking.

After a few pleasantries, Stef thanked his friend and broke contact. Obviously, it was a waste of time talking to anyone; they accepted everything that City Control gave them, and why they should not; City Control's record of control was unblemished. That is it would be without considering Pryme and her apartment, and the unusual appearance of a dinner for two last night! An unwanted appearance, or was it? Elo had said that a malfunction of a food order would be followed by other more complex procedures, such as Pryme's apartment.

He ordered a hot drink and an armchair, and sat and thought some more about what to do. Without seeing the recent aberrations, no one would even consider that something was wrong with City Control. This was to be totally on his shoulders, the responsibility for the life of another. He could not see that Pryme was a threat to anyone, so she could continue as she was, and Stef felt a compulsion for her to do so. That left the problem of his report; how could he complete the task and not involve Pryme? Yes, some regulations had been broken, but was that a sufficient cause to destroy a person? That was wrong! There were no regulations, but Pryme and her surroundings were abnormal, but was that a crime?

The empty cup automatically vanished when empty without his noticing. Deep in thought he wrestled with the problem. Finally, he stirred, "Control Central, information!" He would ask Control, the apparent source of the abnormalities. He had never approached Control Central directly before, the core of everything, so the immediate response was surprising.

"Yes, can I be of assistance Stef?" The voice was soft and mellow, not the plain unemotional one he was expecting, the one that gave him the tasks over the years, City Control. He was not surprised at the use of his name; Control Central knew everything!

"Yes Control! Last night I ordered my usual meal for one, but a large ornate table and dinner for two appeared. Can you explain this?" He held his breath, having now revealed part of his dilemma.

"Was it not pleasing to you?" Control answered.

"That was not the point!" Stef replied, surprised that Control did not give a direct answer. "It was contradictory to the order that I gave. I was alone and only required a simple meal."

Control still did not answer directly, "What else is on your mind Stef? You appear to be confused."

Stef felt intimidated by the question; it was as though Control could read his thoughts. He still felt as though he should protect Pryme, even from Control. "It has never happened before, and I wanted to know why."

There was a long silence, and then Control spoke, "I can find no record of such an event. I can see that you ordered a meal, table and chair, and then you consumed the food. Was it not to your satisfaction?"

Stef was dumbfounded! Was Control avoiding giving an answer, or had it been a figment of his imagination?

"Is there something wrong with your records?" Stef asked.

"Such as?" Control replied.

"That table for two really happened, but you have no record." Stef was getting angry, "Why do you not record it?"

"Are you sure?" Control sounded amused, and that was making Stef even angrier.

"I am positive!" Stef almost shouted.

Again there was a pause before Control answered, "If I were you, I would think this through!"

"It did happen!" Stef did shout this time.

"If you say so," Control answered in a soothing voice, "I would advise you not to lose your temper and think again. A cool head is better for thinking, and perhaps there is a further problem that you have not yet considered."

Stef was stunned! Control had denied that the event happened, and even implied that Stef was having hallucinations! Or did he? Stef calmed down and gathered his thoughts. Control had said that there may be another problem, but not that it was Stef or even Pryme. Was Control trying to steer him in the right direction? Think deeper! Control was trying to help, but it was Stef that had to arrive at the solution and work for it rather than the answer being given on a plate.

The table for two did appear, and that meant that there was another controlling force. He had not heard of one, Control was all, so what could the other element be? He sat down in the armchair again and ordered up an old movie. While that was playing, his subconscious would be working on the problem, but he never saw the end of the movie, he fell asleep!

He dreamed of Pryme. She was walking in her garden, and Ega was with her, but not as a drone; she was a young girl dressed in the same loose garment as Pryme, only Ega's was a soft pink, and they were picking flowers and laughing. Stef remembered an old picture he had seen once, young women in pursuit of some pleasure in a garden, laughing and teasing each other. He had no idea why he thought that the young girl was Ega, but it seemed a natural thought.

He awoke with a start and looked round, half expecting to see the idyllic scene, but the room was bare, a uniform blankness in contrast to the joyful and colourful scene that he had witnessed in his dream. He decided then that the answer to the problem was probably with Pryme, and after further thought, maybe Ega as well! He ordered a bubble and walked to the embarkation point.

CHAPTER FOUR

The long journey seemed to pass swiftly this time, as Stef was immersed in his thoughts and ignoring the passage of time. He almost ran from the bubble, eager to reach Pryme's apartment, but controlled himself on the moving pavement; he would not get there any quicker. The boys of class '08 had tried that once, running on the moving pavement, and it made no difference to the travel time.

At the entrance to Pryme's apartment, his impatience came to a stop; the door would not open! It was some minutes before the door melted away to reveal Ega waiting for him.

"The mistress is asleep!" her pleasant voice informed him.

Stef paused and realised that it was probably in the sleep period. He had failed to account for the travel time in the bubble!

"If you would like to wait in here, I will see if she has woken up." Ega invited him into a side room that he had not noticed before. There was a fragile-looking chair, and he nervously sat down, testing to see if it would bear his weight. It creaked alarmingly but held. Ega had called Pryme mistress, an old fashioned word used by servants. No one had servants today!

He looked around the room. There were pictures on the walls of birds and animals, a flower or two. An apartment with two rooms was unusual, and there must be at least a third where Ega disappeared into. There was no need for more rooms; Control could fashion everything required in a single room. This was another anomaly!

Eventually, Pryme appeared, and apart from her tousled hair, she looked fresh. Her night attire was similar to what she had worn earlier, but so sheer it was almost transparent.

"Good evening Stef," she greeted him, "What do you want at this unexpected hour? Come through, and Ega can fetch some tea, while you can tell us of your errand."

The main room was exactly as it was before, and Stef realised that it had not been produced by Control. Strangely, it felt comfortable to him, and he seated himself on an armchair facing Pryme, who lounged on the sofa; the same armchair and sofa that they had sat in before. He realised that this was the same chair that he had sat on earlier, actually this chair, and not a reproduction. He glanced at the windows, but they were covered with a material carrying a bright pattern, the name of which he could not recall.

He coughed to clear his throat. Ega appeared with a tea-tray and set it down on the small table. Pryme picked up her cup and peered over the brim at him as she sipped, her large grey eyes even wider with an unsaid question. Stef felt his stomach squirm; she was even more beautiful than ever, and he did not regret coming and waking her in the middle of the night.

After sipping his tea, of a strangely aromatic smell and flavour, he coughed again, nervously trying to approach the subject. Pryme's eyes never left his as she continued to sip her tea.

27

"The point is," Stef began, "I have checked the records, and this apartment should not exist in the way it does!"

At last Pryme lowered her cup and set it on the saucer. "Well, it does as you can see. What is the problem?"

"All of the apartments were set by City Control," Stef explained, "Any alterations must be approved and recorded. Without approval, the whole structure of the City could be thrown out of balance, and there are no records of any apartment being open to the sky. You have uncontrolled access to the upper surface and more rooms than you really require. You also have the use of personal drones, and they provide artefacts instead of City Control. It is almost as though you do not belong to the City!"

Pryme gave a soft sigh, "So that is the problem! City Control did not give permission, but he must have done, it is here, and I did not alter it!" she stated the obvious.

"There is also the problem of Ega being your personal drone." Stef felt uncomfortable; these questions seemed out of place. "And that she makes artefacts," he waved at the table and wall ornaments.

"She is not just a drone, she is my friend, and why shouldn't she make things?" Pryme shrugged, "It amuses her and pleases me!"

The thought that a drone could be amused sounded strange. "No one else has a personal drone, and all manufacturing has to be approved by City Control." Stef felt that his words were meaningless even as he uttered them.

"Are you jealous?" Pryme's lips compressed in a tight smile, "Would you like an apartment like this?"

Stef laughed, "Jealous! Why an earth would I be jealous? It is a matter of rules!"

"City Control's rules!" Pryme snorted. "Why are those rules important?"

Stef was aghast, "Without rules the world would descend into chaos!"

"Is that a bad thing?" Pryme stood up and whirled around, the garment flaring open to revealing her brown limbs, "Is there a rule that says that I should not dance, or sing, or be happy? Are there rules that say that Ega cannot do these things?"

"No – no, don't be ridiculous!" Stef felt his temperature rising as his eyes were captivated by Pryme's beauty.

Pryme suddenly sat down, "So what is the problem?" She stood again and reached over to take his hand, "Come with me!"

The material covering the windows had disappeared, and Stef realised that the sun was absent. The light from the room lit the flowers for a short distance, and then after that there was nothing but the night. For a moment his courage failed him, but Pryme's insistent joy and tugging overcame his reluctance, barefoot she stepped on to the grass without hesitation. He followed her into the enchantment of a starlit garden.

His reluctance of being in the open vanished as he tilted his head and looked up to the sky open mouthed, half expecting that it would still be raining, but there were no clouds. Above them was an arc of scintillating lights, and on either side, there was a scattering of other lights. These are stars! His mind was engulfed with the vision; against the dark sky they stood out in twinkling contrast, thousands, millions of distant points of light!

The next thing that he knew was that he was lying on the damp grass with Pryme anxiously stooped over him, and something warm and wet was brushing his face. He sat up and recoiled in horror; the thing that was touching his face was an animal! He frantically wiped his face on his sleeve. The animal looked up as he scrambled to his feet, still backing away from the creature. Its tongue was hanging out, and it was panting. Obviously, the creature had been licking him, and at that thought, he almost threw up.

"That's Benza!" Pryme informed him, "It's a dog."

Stef had never seen any animal in real life, and as far as he knew, all animals had died out centuries ago. There was no place for them in the scheme of things, but he had seen on films that they were often depicted as faithful companions.

"Where did you get that?" He realised that his voice squeaked as he asked.

Pryme pointed out into the darkness, "Out there! The poor thing was lost. He won't hurt you!" To prove it, she knelt down and fondled its ears, and in response Benza reared up and licked her face. For a moment, Stef thought that it was attacking her.

Pryme stood and looked at him questioningly, "Are you feeling better? You fainted when you looked up at the sky."

Instinctively, Stef looked up again. The stars were still there, silent witnesses to this little scenario. He dragged his eyes away and looked at this strange woman who lived in the open and had drones and animals, no, he corrected himself, dogs for friends. She must be the anomaly that he was sent to investigate. The question was 'what was she doing that was wrong?'

He looked up at the sky nervously. The stars were still there, and as he looked, a streak of light fled from one side of the sky to the other. He realised that he understood as much about them as he did of Pryme and her odd collection of friends. Control Central had intimated that there was another question hidden here, but Stef had too many questions about everything, and his mind was overloaded.

"In an hour or two, the moon will rise, and that transforms everything!" Pryme said, "There are many legends about the moon, and the stars. You should study them!"

Stef stiffened, "That is archaic nonsense! We do not even tell those tales to the children!"

"Oh, so you have heard those stories!" Pryme quietly laughed, "If you know that they are archaic, you must have heard them! You gave yourself away Stef!"

Stef was flustered, "Maybe I did long ago when I was a child, but they are never discussed in polite circles."

"Are they banned?" Pryme sat down on the grass with her hands on her knees, seemingly oblivious of the damp condition of the grass.

Stef had no idea if the stories were banned, "They are not banned, just not approved of. They are not suitable for adults!"

"Ah! Who is it that disapproves?" Pryme appeared to be almost playing a game.

"Society!" Stef stated firmly.

"What is society Stef? Who are these people who disapprove of harmless stories?" Without waiting for an answer, Pryme turned to Ega, who was still standing in the window, "Shall we tell of distant days, of heroes, and maidens? Shall we tell stories of fabulous creatures and hidden treasures? Ega, be a dear and fetch some punch so that we can celebrate the night."

"This is far too much..." Stef started to object, but Pryme cut him off.

"It is no trouble at all! Ega likes to do things, and the punch will soften the night, making the stories come to life."

"I was referring to your lack of responsibility!" Stef said sternly.

Pryme raised her eyebrows, her large grey eyes seemingly like the shadows of thoughts. Stef could swear that he could see the reflection of stars in their depths. Despite the objections, Ega returned with a large ornate crystal bowl, on the rim of which hung two crystal glasses.

"Oh, you are a sweetheart!" Pryme patted the lawn, "Set it down here, and I'll serve," She filled one glass from a crystal ladle, the two making a musical note as they met, and handed it up to Stef, which, with a slight hesitation, he accepted. Then she filled her own.

"Sit down here Stef, as you're making my neck stiff!" Stef did as he was bid, and Pryme raised her glass.

"Here is to the stories of yesteryear, may they never die!" She clinked her glass to his and took a sip, her eyes never moving from his. Stef had no choice but to take a sip.

The sensation produced by the taste was immediate; it was like an explosion in his mouth and his eyes watered. There was a dullness in his hearing, and through that he heard music and saw Ega playing an instrument, a large triangle that contained beams of light, and when she touched these there was a musical notes that filled the air and his mind.

"There were times that people believed in gods and fairies, and men doing heroic deeds," Pryme began to tell the stories, "All of the women were young and beautiful, and the men sought them as well as the gods. There was magic in the trees and the sky, and miracles were common-place."

CHAPTER FIVE

Stef awoke suddenly. It was totally dark, and for a brief moment, he thought that he was blind. His apartment, and of all others, would retain a low level of luminance during sleep periods, and this total absence of light was unnerving, but as he moved, a source of light dimly illuminated the room. It was not his room!

The bed that he lay on had four posts that held a canopy over his head, and by the side of the bed was a small table with a glass of clear liquid. Around the room there were pictures on the walls, strange cabinets with ornaments were stationed in a regular order, and there was one of those windows, now covered with that material, which Stef now recalled was called a curtain. He could only be in Pryme's apartment, and then the memory of last night came to his mind.

He remembered the beginning of the night. The drink was powerfully scented, and it caught his throat as he swallowed, making him gag and cough. After gaining his composure, he took a second sip, and found that it was warming; he could feel a tingle down to his toes. Pryme was watching him, those large grey eyes enveloping the scene.

"Ega says that this is a very old recipe, and I have no idea of where she found it, but I have the most wondrous feeling when I drink it, and outside seems to be the right place to be when it is drunk." Pryme swung her head and her dark hair cascaded over her shoulders.

It certainly did appear to counteract the cool night air. Stef could feel his cheeks glowing with warmth, but his voice had disappeared! He coughed a few times, but every time he tried to say something, all he could manage was a dry rasp. He took a second glass, by which time Pryme's face was all that he could see, filling the universe, or at least his part of it. From somewhere soft music could be heard, soothing notes and chords that matched the night, the moment, and Pryme's grey eyes. After that, he could remember nothing!

He threw off the light cover and swung his legs over the edge of the bed. He was naked! That was normal, and then he realised that City Control had automatically removed them when he fell asleep.

"City Control! Please supply a coverall." His mouth was dry, and the instruction was hoarse and scratchy, so he reached for the glass and took a sip. No coverall had arrived! Frowning, he ordered again in a firmer voice, but still nothing appeared. There was a movement behind him, and he turned to see that Ega had entered the room unannounced. Stef drew the cover over himself, not to cover his nakedness, but because a drone should not have been there and he felt uncomfortable.

"If Stef is ready, I have these clothes for him." She held out some material. Stef reached for them and realised that it was not a coverall. Instead, it consisted of two garments, one for the upper body and the other for the lower half. In Ega's other hand were a pair of foot coverings. He smiled his thanks but felt awkward to dress in front of the drone.

"Thank you Ega, I'll be out shortly." He dismissed her.

"The mistress is waiting at the breakfast table," Ega said. Again that antiquated reference to Pryme.

He sighed when the drone turned and glided out of the room. He held up the garments and saw that they lacked the perfectly smooth finish of the coveralls. Instead, they had a fine pattern. With a shock, Stef realised that these had been made by Ega from raw materials! Another departure from the norm was the vivid colours, blue and yellow.

After requesting a shower and none appeared, with his skin crawling at the thought of microbes, he donned the trousers and shirt, trying all the time not to think of the microscopic life that may be in them. The foot coverings were made of some tough material in several sections, but when he slipped them on, they were warm and comfortable. Suitably attired, he made his way into the main room and saw Pryme and Ega at a table outside. On seeing him, Pryme waved him to come outside. He found that the shoes, he remembered the name, were ideal for walking on the grass, but the garments were tight without the give of a coverall.

"Good morning Stef!" Pryme greeted him, "Those clothes suit you very well! Now, what would you like for breakfast?" Without asking, she poured out a steaming hot beverage into a large plain cup.

"I usually eat porridge in the mornings," he said as he sat down on a sturdy looking chair. A wooden chair that creaked he noticed.

"Ega, be a sweet and fetch Stef some porridge, and I'll have some too, and some juice." Pryme gave Stef a beaming smile, "Did you sleep well?"

Stef nodded, "What happened last night? I remember the drink; you were telling tales and that there was some music, but after that nothing!"

"We danced!" Pryme said, "You have a natural sense of rhythm, did you know that? Then we talked until quite late, and then you fell asleep. I find that the punch can do that, especially if you are not used to it."

"We danced!" Stef had no recollection of the event, and as far as he could remember, he had never danced with anyone before!

Pryme nodded, "Several times, and then you said that you wanted to sit down, so then we talked."

"Who put me to bed?" Stef asked.

"Ega! She is quite strong, and then she made those clothes for you." Pryme pointed to the upper cover, "That colour suits you well. Do you like them?"

"They are a bit tight!" Stef complained.

"Oh, that is normal, but after a day or two they will take on your shape," Pryme informed him, and he was struck by the peculiar and disgusting thought of wearing clothes twice!

Pryme looked up as Ega appeared with a tray of food. "Oh, you are a dear! And you brought the sugar. We didn't know if you like the porridge sweet or not."

Stef looked at the brown flakes in the bowl. The porridge he usually ate was a plain grey product, not this rich brown colour. He watched as Pryme poured a white liquid over her porridge, and then scooped out of another bowl some white crystals, which she sprinkled over her porridge. He copied her actions and found that the taste burst in his mouth, so much so that for a moment he just sucked on the contents of his mouth. He had never tasted anything with such strong flavours.

After swallowing, he reached for the glass of juice, slightly green in colour. The flavour also hit him powerfully; his eyes watered as the taste buds on his tongue burst into life, probably the first time in his life.

Pryme monitored his reactions, "That is real food, from out there!" she pointed to the lakes and hills. For a moment, Stef's reaction was to spit out the juice, and then with further consideration; he swallowed it.

"For a moment I felt nauseated," he said, "and then I thought, 'why should I object to these wonderful flavours!' I suspect that poisons could be just as tasty."

"We can go down and see where these things grow when you have finished eating," Pryme said and smiled at his obvious pleasure.

"I would like to do that," Stef said through a large mouthful, "What surprises me is that this stuff still grows on the Outside!"

"There is so much growing out there, that we do not know what to do with it, or how!" Pryme informed him. Ega brought in another tray with two cups and a huge pot of coffee, and when the flavour of that hit Stef's tongue, his eyes watered again.

CHAPTER SIX

The path that led down to the ocean shore was an adventure! Pryme kept diving off the path, dragging him into the lush undergrowth to show him a small flower or some peculiar object that she insisted was a fruit. She plucked one round red and green fruit and took a mouthful.

"Taste it!" she urged and held the fruit towards him, "Ega says that it is an apple".

At first, he declined the offer, and then he took the fruit and bit into it. Immediately the tangy flavour burst in his mouth, and he bent forward to allow the juice to drop from his chin onto the grass and soil. Pryme laughed at his surprised expression.

"This tastes the same as the drink!" Stef mumbled through the mouthful.

Pryme gave a tinkling laugh, "It was the juice from the apple that we had for breakfast!"

Not only did Stef take mental notes of the things that he was shown, he thought that Pryme was the most alive person he had ever known, and he took mental notes of her joy at living. She ran barefoot through the grass, her hair streaming behind. This was Pryme's World, not that blank and featureless corridors within the City where everyone else in civilisation lived.

In this gentle but wild abandoned way, they reached the shoreline. Stef had never seen such a vast amount of water. It reflected the sun's rays, at times creating brilliant pinpoints of light scintillating on the crests of the waves, and it was forever moving, like a restless animal prowling the confines of its cage.

Pryme took his arm and stared towards the horizon. "Ega tells me that this is only a lake, not even a sea or ocean. Can you imagine something as large as an ocean?"

"Do you talk to Ega a lot?" Stef asked, pulling her arm into his side.

"Well, apart from you, there is no one else!" She said.

That surprised Stef, he was always checking in with the class of '08, and some of his work colleagues, and there was always City Control. He could not imagine a day passing without making contact with someone. Then he remembered the lack of detail in her file, and that would account for her isolation.

Above their heads, something gave out a shrill cry, and Stef involuntary looked up. There were two creatures wheeling and hovering over the lake, and he remembered that at one time there were birds and other flying creatures. As he brought his gaze down to the lake, he saw the same creatures were floating on the surface. He paused in thought; there appeared to be many dimensions, if that was the right word, to Pryme's World, far more than he was exposed to in his world.

"How long has Ega been with you?" Stef asked.

"I can't remember a time when she was not with me, so it must have been very early in my life." Pryme had removed her arm from his grip and stepped barefoot into the water. Stef had never seen her wearing shoes of any sort.

"Be careful!" he warned her, "You may hurt your feet!"

"Don't be silly!" she said turning to him with a smile, "Take those things off and enjoy the sensation of clean water and soft sand; you would be surprised just how refreshing it is."

Stef mentally recoiled at the thought of stepping into the water, it could be deep in places, and as if she had read his mind, Pryme moved further out until the water reached her knees, and then she stooped and threw a handful of water at him.

He flinched as the water struck his face, but it was surprisingly warm and gentle. Seeing his reluctance to join in her game, Pryme waded on to the shore.

"You do not know what you are missing!" she stated, and Stef just gave a soft grunt of disbelief. She took his arm again, and they walked along the shore. They spent the afternoon exploring the world in the Outside.

CHAPTER SEVEN

Stef had broken away from the spell that Pryme had weaved over him during the day and returned to his apartment. Her magic was working, as he entered his room, he felt a sense of dread and depression. There was no life here!

He requested that one wall should become a window revealing the surface above. He stared in horror and disbelief as the picture appeared. It was not the green paradise that he had seen and expected as at Pryme's garden, there were no plants, just a steaming rocky surface, devoid of even a single blade of grass! The depression hit him at sight, like a blow to the head, and he asked for a change to somewhere that was green and pleasant. To his surprise, he found himself looking at Pryme's garden, but from a different angle. The depressed feeling left him instantly! He recalled the length of the journey, and obviously his apartment was far away from Pryme's, and the surface above him was not the green haven of her garden.

He then ordered a comfortable armchair and a small side table, adding that he wanted them to remain at all times, even when he was absent. A degree of comfort had entered his home, although it was a far cry from the feeling he had when at Pryme's.

He settled himself in the armchair and ordered a hot drink, and then changed it instantly to being specific, a hot coffee. That was what he had seen in those old movies. It had a bitter-sweet taste that enervated him, so he started to go over the events of the past few days.

Unfortunately, the coffee turned out to be an insipid substitute for Ega's coffee.

City Control had sent him on this mission to investigate an anomaly, and the anomaly was Pryme! And it was also City Control! Only City Control could have built that apartment and attached the drones unless the drones had built the apartment, but City Control would have had to have given them the order to do so. If that was the case, then the anomaly was City Control, and that meant that City Control wanted itself to be investigated!

It still did not explain Pryme's odd behaviour. Any one of his friends would have run away from that apartment and its view of the outside world, but she had accepted it, even became a part of it! If City Control had created the apartment, was it also responsible for Pryme? What had Pryme been doing during those curiously blank years? Although he had been sent to investigate the anomaly, every time it was Pryme that had led the conversation. Stef had lost control simply because Pryme's world was so different to what he had become accustomed to.

Then there was the odd appearance of the dining table for two in his apartment, and when questioned, Control Central had denied all knowledge of the incident. If anything, that was more worrying to Stef than Pryme's apartment! For centuries, Control Central had built the City, and everything had run like clockwork, until now. His old friend Elia had dismissed the idea that there was anything wrong with City

Control, but what would he say if he had seen the table and Pryme's apartment? He would probably quickly refute it!

Stef needed to talk this over with someone, but it could not be Elo, or Control, or Pryme, but he felt the need to bounce ideas off someone, so he spent a few hours, and drank more of the insipid coffee, thinking of who he could confide in, and would accept his suspicions. His thoughts were interrupted by a call signal.

There was a slight hesitation between Stef's acceptance of the call and the appearance of a jovial, plump man in a holographic image. He was seated at an old piece of furniture that Stef remembered was a called a secretary. The man sat sideways to this, and he had a book open on the secretary's lid, and that was curious, no one read books anymore!

"Are you Officer Stef Barak?" the plump man asked anxiously, "I am Jol, and City Control has instructed me to contact you."

Control again! "What else did Control say?" Stef asked.

"Nothing! I assumed that you would know why." Jol blinked owlishly.

"Then tell me what you do, and perhaps that would shed some light." Stef was becoming tired of this guessing game that Control appears to have given him.

"I am a historian," Jol said.

Stef did not know that there were historians any more, it was one of those subjects that were dismissed as unimportant. What would a historian supply to Stef about this current problem? Control obviously thought there was something, or was this another error?

"Just at the moment, I cannot think of why Control has asked you to contact me," Stef said lamely.

"I have been studying the history of the city, and I have found it most interesting. Would that be of use to you?" Jol said eagerly. He was reminded of Pryme's puppy.

"I have been researching the files, but only in a limited way, just recent events. Perhaps that is what has triggered Control to connect us." Stef ventured a guess.

"Oh, undoubtedly that is the reason." Jol nodded his head, "What exactly have you been researching?"

Stef hesitated. He was still reluctant to reveal the presence of Pryme to outsiders. "What I have been researching is the pattern of building within the city, how the construction and layout were arrived at. Would that be something in your line?"

Jol's head nearly came off as he rapidly nodded, "Indeed it is, and I can be of assistance to you."

What struck Stef was the terribly old-fashioned speech that Jol used, over polite. He could almost be a historical figure. Jol had turned to the secretary and was pulling out rolls of paper from its interior. The paper was not used today, although Control could produce it, it was more convenient to transmit to a reading wall section that was installed everywhere. Stef had only once seen real paper in his early years in the class of '08. Jol was more old-fashioned in many ways!

"I have here the original layout of the city if you would care to look at it." Jol had unrolled a sheet of paper and offered it to Stef.

Stef instinctively reached for the paper, and then snorted, "I cannot read it like this! Can you transmit it?" It was only an image that could not be handled.

"Oh, er, yes, of course, silly me!" Jol looked flustered as he rolled up the paper. "You could ask Control for a copy, but I only recently found this with great difficulty, and I am sure that it does not exist in City Control's archives."

That was something new to Stef; something that was not in Control's files, and Jol did not appear to see that it was odd. Not really believing it, Stef called to City Control.

"I am sorry Stef," City Control said after several seconds, "There appears to be little of the earliest days of the city in my files. I will search further, but I do not think that I will find anything of value."

Stef sat frozen in shocked surprise. He would have to take up the matter with Elo at a later time, but as at present, he was staring into the slightly comical face of Jol.

"We come across this all too often," Jol smiled apologetically, although it was not his fault.

"We?" Stef questioned.

"Oh yes, there are quite a number of historians, and we are always running into dead-ends," Jol explained.

"So where did you find that, and how do you transfer your finds?" Stef was becoming curious about Jol and his friends, and the strange life that they led, and then he thought, 'another strange person, another anomaly!'

"I found this in the archives, and if I want to share this with another historian, we have to meet. If it is of great interest, then a copy is made." Jol explained.

"How do you copy it?" Stef half expected the answer, but it was still a surprise when Jol revealed the method.

"We use paper and ink!" Jol held the paper aloft to prove his statement.

"Where are these archives?" Stef asked.

"I can give you the co-ordinates, and we can meet there," Jol said eagerly.

"No, not at the moment," Stef held up his hand to quell Jol's eagerness, "I think that first I would like to see what you have collected, and then we can progress from there."

Jol spread his hands, "You are most welcome, but it may mean little to you without becoming familiarised with this type of work."

"Then you can explain it to me! Would tomorrow be convenient?" Stef asked, and broke the connection when Jol agreed.

Stef's mind was in a whirl! What was going on? Pryme, her apartment, the drones, the garden, and now historians and an unknown secret archives, at least unknown to Stef, and records that were not contained in City Controls extensive files. That last thought worried Stef very much!

CHAPTER EIGHT

Jol's apartment was close to his own; the bubble hardly had time to get up to speed before he arrived at his destination. On disembarking, the moving pavement travelled down a slope, two of them, and Stef had the impression that he was deep under the City. This was confirmed when the moving pavement stopped, and he had to walk along the last corridor. Of course, Stef should have realised that by the address that was in Section Three, one of the oldest in the City, and moving pavements were not invented until well after the City was started.

Jol met him at the door. A short, tubby man, who bowed him politely into the apartment. Pryme's apartment he had found startling, and so was Jol's, but in a different way. On the walls hung paintings, old maps, and several documents, all framed and displayed in a regular pattern. In between the frames were odd small pictures and scraps of paper, real paper! At one end was the secretary that was festooned with odd files and papers, and at the other end of the room was a chest and a table, absolutely cluttered with all manner of things. Jol was a very untidy person!

Lifting some books from a chair, Jol bid him sit, and inquired if he needed refreshment. Stef's first impulse was to decline the offer, but then he changed his mind.

"I will have some coffee if you don't mind." Stef was relieved when two cups materialised; at least this part of Jol's life was normal!

"Coffee is very interesting to historians," Jol said as he sat opposite Stef, "It was coffee that caused the

Great Enlightenment." He said that as if it was of great importance.

"I'm sorry, what enlightenment?" Stef asked, bewildered by the term.

"That was when we began to understand how the universe worked," Jol's head was nodding again, "Coffee was discovered and was for sale in coffee houses, and it was so popular that people met in the coffee houses and exchanged ideas," Jol sighed, "It must have been a wonderful time when all the world was new!"

"When was this?" Despite this was not anything to do with his quest, Stef was curious.

"Oh, a long time ago, long before the City was even thought of," Jol said firmly, "but there must have been a city of some sorts even then. We historians keep caching glimpses on old films and documents."

"I have seen some of those old films," Stef admitted, "it looked a chaotic kind of life."

"I'm sure that it was!" Jol nodded, "Some of us are trying to establish how it worked, what sort of systems of management they used. Now we just have City Control."

"Yes, now we have City Control," Stef agreed and thought if Jol had any inkling that City Control was possibly not the awesome power that everyone thought.

"But you did not come for that!" Jol rolled open the paper he had previously waved at Stef, "This is one of the earliest drawings of the City, but by this time it had already been growing for some time."

Stef studied the lines on the paper, he felt the fragile material and wondered how it had survived. The drawing showed five views of the City, an overhead plan, and side views. By the time that this drawing was produced, the City was already five or six levels deep.

"What is that?" Stef's finger jabbed at a line wandering by the side of the City.

"That I believe is a river," Jol explained, "We believe that it led to a lake that is on another roll." He rummaged around in the secretary and produced another roll.

It covered a larger area, and it was of a later time, the City was larger, but it has still not reached the shores of the lake. This must be the lake where Pryme had walked in the water; there were no signs of another lake, so this must be it!

"What are these?" His finger followed some meandering lines, "Are they more rivers?"

"It took a long time to find out what they were, but we have definite proof that these were roads!" Jol said. They did not look like roads to Stef; they curved in different directions, meandering across the ground.

"They do not look like roads," Stef frowned, "They could not have attained any speed with all of these bends!"

"That was what confused us at first, but they had primitive vehicles that could stop and start anywhere they wanted to, and did not travel at very high speed." Jol did not sound impressed at the mode of transport, but only in that it had existed.

"Not very practical," Stef confirmed both of their thoughts, "These lines appear to be straighter. Are you sure that these are roads and not the other?"

"They are railroads, used for hauling heavy freight," Jol said, "Those vehicles were larger and much more powerful. There were networks of roads and railroads everywhere."

Stef studied the drawing for some minutes before asking his next question.

"How did they live at the oldest time, as on the first drawing? Did they have access to the outside?"

Jol looked up at Stef in astonishment," Oh, I would not have thought so! The whole purpose of the City was to keep the inhabitants safe inside."

"Then can you explain how they got in and out of the vehicles, and what did they do when they stopped here, for example?" Stef's finger rested on the line of a road far outside of the City.

Jol looked dumbfounded, and then he stuttered, "I- I see what you mean." He rushed over to the table and furiously sorted through some papers.

"Here it is!" He triumphantly held up a small piece of paper, "This is what they travelled in, they called it an automobile."

Stef took the paper and found that it was a photograph on a stiff card. It showed a man and a woman in peculiar clothes, standing in front of a four-wheeled vehicle. The important point was that they would sit in the Open, exposed to the elements.

Jol was very excited, "We thought that it was taken inside the City, you can see the buildings behind them, but there may be no cover over the City at that time. Everyone was exposed to the Open!"

"I am certain by looking at this drawing, that they were exposed for most of the time." Stef pointed to the open spaces outside of the City confines. He remembered some of the old movies, vehicles stuck in mud while rain pelted down from the sky. Then he remembered one where the actor was dancing in the rain. They must have enjoyed it, but he could not see how, and he shuddered at the thought! Then he remembered the experience in Pryme's garden, and the rain did not appear to be that awful! He looked again at the photograph and realised that the woman's dress was similar in a way to Pryme's, it flowed over her body, and her arms, legs, and shoulders were bare. He peered closer.

"Are these people white or brown?" he asked.

Jol took the photograph back and produced a magnifying glass, the first that Stef had ever seen, which he peered through, "I never thought of it before, but they look darker than you and me."

"Would exposure to the wind and rain cause the skin to darken?" Stef asked.

Jol thought for a moment, his hand on his chin, then he walked to the desk and opened a draw, and after a moment produced a folder.

"We found these, but they make no sense to any of us." He handed the folder to Stef. The folder contained a few garish pictures of semi-naked men and women, and completely naked in a few cases, with bold letters across the page. Stef tried to read the words, but the language was archaic, so he handed the problem to Jol.

"'Have a tan all year', this one says, 'enjoy the healthy look of a fit person', 'sun-beds available twenty-four hours'." Jol read in short bursts as he deciphered the words.

Stef nodded, "It appears that the sun and weather can darken the skin, and at that time they thought that this was a sign of good health." That explained Pryme's dark skin; she had spent considerable time outside, probably as much as the people in the photograph.

"Seems a bit barbaric to me!" complained Jol.

Stef made up his mind to trust the historian, at least in part, "Do you know of any part of the City that is open as it must have been in those days?"

"Open! Good Golly no!" Jol looked horrified, his jowls wobbling as he shook his head, "That could expose all of us to unknown hazards. City Control would not allow it!"

"Alright, try this! Have you come across any reference to City Control doing something odd?" Stef held his breath.

"No, no!" Jol burst out, "That is unthinkable! If that…" he stopped with his finger on his fat lower lip. Something was stirring in the back of his mind. "I will have to check on something if I can find it, but I have a question for you. Do you suspect that there is an opening in the City?"

Here was the moment! Stef took a deep breath, "I know that there is, and I think that City Control created it, but why it did is the big question. I also suspect that it will produce no harm to any of us inside."

Jol looked at Stef with a strange expression, "You have been in the Outside!" It was not a question; he knew with a certainty, and he spoke in awe.

Stef nodded, "I have, but I still need to know why City Control made the opening. See if you can find out why, and I will check from my end. I will check with you in a few days."

CHAPTER NINE

In the quiet of his room, Stef thought through what he had found out. Control must have a reason, but Stef will have to discover that for himself. Pryme was simply an entertaining signpost on that journey, and an attractive one! Or was there more to her?

The room looked more comfortable than before; he added a sideboard, some ornaments for that, and some pictures of animals on the walls. Now he added curtains for his window, and a rug for the floor. It resembled the rooms that he had seen on the movies. He settled down and looked through his 'window'.

It was definitely Pryme's garden, he could follow the path down to the lake, and the stand of tall trees were identical. Why had City Control selected that particular scene for his window? He started! This was in real-time, for there was Pryme walking down that path, and by her side was a young girl, skipping through the long grasses. He knew it was Ega, but if this was in real-time, why was he being shown the drone as a young girl as in his dream? Had City Control read his dreams? Could City Control read minds? The dog Benza was racing back and forth, circling them in an obvious show of energy and affection as he played a dog's game.

They were collecting flowers, and some of them they placed in their hair like jewelled crowns. Stef felt like calling out or even stepping through the 'window', but he realised that it would prove fatal, so he contented himself with watching the two girls at play. The scene tugged at his heart; it seemed so natural, and he felt a deep longing. After some time the sky darkened, and the two women returned home.

With a shake of his head, Stef turned his mind with some difficulty to his set task. What he had seen so far was a message, but he had not discovered how to read it, and he suspected that the message was far from complete. Was City Control asking for help? If it was, it was a devious method!

It was too late now, by the time that he got to her apartment, she would be long asleep, and so he set the alarm to bring him to Pryme's for breakfast. He knew that he would not get much sleep, but as it turned out, he hardly had any at all. After showering and settling in bed, his mind would not shut off. Jol had shown him a lot to think about, and for a few moments he imagined the people in the photograph, climbing into the open car and speeding off on twisting and winding roads, the wind in their hair, and they would be laughing. He sat bolt upright in bed.

"City Control! Can you produce the earliest image of the City in your records and the surrounding area?" he asked.

Without making a remark, City Control produced a shimmering 3D image in the middle of the room. It was almost as it was today, but he could clearly see the lake and a river coming out of the City that flowed into the lake. He asked to be shown Section ??356-12-54992, Pryme's apartment, and a small glowing spot appeared above and outside of the existing buildings. Pryme's apartment had not been built when this image was taken. He then ordered a current image with Pryme's apartment, and there it was, one of the last apartments to be built, at the edge of the City, and it was not open to the outside. He studied it for a long time before sleep came for a brief period.

When he awoke, the scene at his window was dark, but he could see the twinkle of a few stars. He ordered a breakfast that he remembered from an old movie, ham and eggs, some toast, coffee and orange juice. He had no idea what ham, eggs, or orange juice were, but they tasted just awful, but his stomach rumbled as it experienced this food for the first time. After that, he dressed in the clothes that Pryme had given to him earlier. If he had met anyone on his journey, this costume would create some remarks, but there would be no one to see him in the grey corridors or the tunnels, apart from drones, and they would not ask.

Through the long journey, he ran over his thoughts, but above that he felt an anticipation of the meeting to come. He intended to spend a long time there and persuade Pryme and Ega to explore the area with him. It seemed important that Ega should be part of this, and perhaps he would discover why City Control insisted in showing her as a young girl. He also felt that he should not at first mention that he had a view of her garden, and that he had seen them picking flowers; that could come later when he understood a little more.

He was met at the door by Ega and Benza. He was still nervous of the dog, but its wagging tail seemed to show that the dog was pleased to see him. Pryme was waiting for him in the garden, seated on a rough wooden bench alongside an equally rough wooden table.

"This is how our ancestors would sit in the country, a simple meal on a simple table." Her hair was tied up in some complicated fashion, and she had flowers in her hair. She patted the seat next to her. Stef found that he was not that hungry; it would appear that the substantial but tasteless breakfast that he had was very filling, however, he tackled a dish of fruit and a fruit drink just for the taste.

"I have been looking at some scenes from when they first started building the City," he informed her. Her eyebrows rose with an unspoken question. "That's it, nothing more," he finished.

"What did you think?" Pryme asked.

"It is all so confusing," he said, "There was a different culture then, and trying to understand it is difficult."

"Why?" she asked.

"Well, there didn't appear to be any rules, little or no organisation, people did as they pleased, without any thought of the consequences." Stef stumbled over his explanation; it was so difficult to put into words.

"Do you mean that they were free?" Pryme had a twinkle in her eye, a bright one like those reflections on the lake.

Stef nodded, "Free most certainly, but the harm that they could cause to others, as well as themselves. I am not sure that is a good thing. Perhaps that was why the City was built."

Pryme gave him an opening, "What do you want to do today?"

"I would like to see a bit more of the outside, around the edges of the City," he said.

"I am not sure that there is an edge!" her answer surprised him.

"But I have seen a chart of the City, and you are situated on edge and near the lake," he said.

"Maybe, or maybe not!" Pryme said, "You could have interpreted the chart incorrectly!"

Stef paused, trying to summon the chart into his mind's eye, then he shook his head, "No, I am certain that it is correct!"

"We shall see then!" was all that Pryme said.

"I would like Ega to come with us," Stef added.

"Of course, and Benza too. He does love to run!" Pryme called the dog and Ega, "Stef is going to take us on a walk! Which way do you want to go?"

Stef paused for a moment. He looked down to the lake, and then over the top of Pryme's apartment to the distant mountain peak, the top of the City.

"I think that I would like to go up there." He pointed to the distant white top of the mountain.

Pryme shook her head, but it was Ega who spoke, "That is a long way off, further than it looks, and it would take you more than one day to get there, and that white stuff is ice, frozen water. You are not dressed for such an adventure."

With his mouth open in amazement, Stef stared up at the peak again. It did not look that far. "Why is the water frozen?"

"Because it becomes colder the higher you climb." Ega said.

That did not make sense to Stef, but he gestured towards the lake, "Then we will go this way. Is there anything that I have not seen?"

"The Outside is huge, so you have hardly seen anything!" Pryme informed him, "Even Ega and I have not seen anything beyond this valley and lake." That was a sobering thought!

"I think that there is something that Stef should see," said Ega, "I think that he would be interested in the river." She led the way down to the lake and then walked in the opposite direction to that which Pryme and Stef had taken previously.

The soft sand changed to small pebbles, and Stef could hear a rumble in the distance. Ega chose a path that led upwards and above the lake, the noise becoming louder as they climbed. It became a deafening roar when they rounded some boulders and bushes. Before Stef was a steep drop, and down that a torrent of water poured into the lake. Stef tried to ask questions, but it was impossible for him to be heard. Pryme signalled that they should climb higher, and as they did, the sound diminished until it was a distant murmur.

"What was that?" he asked.

"That was the river," Pryme told him, "Come a little further, and you will see it before it reaches the waterfall." A little way further and they reached the bank of a river. It streamed past on its way to reach the lake. Like the lake, it appeared to Stef that it was a living creature.

"It never stops?" he asked.

"Not as long as the City lives," Pryme said, "This is just one of many outflows from the City. This is the water that is used by the City for all manner of things, and fresh water is drawn from the far side of the lake."

"This is used, dirty water?" Stef's nose wrinkled.

"No! This water has been processed and cleaned before being discharged," Pryme stooped, and taking some water in her hand, drank it. "It would not do to pollute the lake, for that is where we take fresh water."

"How do you know this?" Stef asked.

"Ega told me! She is a fountain of knowledge," Pryme burst out laughing, "That was funny! River and fountain!" she turned towards the lake, and Stef turned with her. They were far above the level of her apartment, and the view was magnificent!

"Why would anyone not want to see this?" Pryme said, "Why would anyone wish to spoil such natural beauty?"

Stef had to agree! Now that they had climbed a short distance, the wind brought the smell of the plants and trees, sweet, tangy, sour, all of them mixed together. The wind ruffled Stef's hair, and Pryme's simple garment fluttered. Standing there, Stef could well imagine that she was nature herself.

CHAPTER TEN

They spent the whole day wandering around the lake, and it was after some hours that Stef realised something. He turned to Pryme and asked a very ordinary question, one that he should have asked before.

"How were these paths made?" he gestured to the trampled grass and soil beneath their feet.

Pryme followed his finger and then turned to Ega as though she had passed the question to her.

"They are made by feet constantly wearing the vegetation down," Ega supplied the answer, but Stef was ready for his next question.

"There are many paths, and it would take a great number of feet, constantly walking here to prevent the grass from growing. Who else walks these paths?" Stef stood waiting for an answer with his hands on his hips.

"There are the drones of course," Ega said, "Without their attention, this would become an impossible wilderness, and then there are the animals."

Stef looked at Benza, "How many of these dogs are there?"

"Over the whole area there are a few, but there are other creatures as well," Ega informed him, "There are several large herds of deer and bison, and then there are the predators, such as Benza here, who prey on the deer."

Stef looked at Benza with an apprehensive expression on his face, "Benza is a predator?" On hearing his name, the dog came over to him with its tail wagging, and for the first time, Stef noticed the large fangs.

"He is only a puppy now, a juvenile, but when he becomes full-size, he will want to hunt just like the other dogs." Pryme appeared unconcerned that a killer was licking her hand.

"Will he attack you?" Stef was horrified.

"It is possible, but we feed him, love him, and that should be enough to prevent any attack!" Ega said. "We are family!" That notion appeared odd to Stef, a human, a drone, and a dog as one family.

Stef looked around their position some distance from the lake. They were standing in a clearing, surrounded by some bushes with yellow flowers, and beyond them were trees with wide spaces between the trunks. What if there were animals watching them now, stalking and waiting for the right moment! Stef felt an involuntary shudder run through him.

Pryme noticed it, and the increase in perspiration on his face, so she slid her cool arm into his.

"You are perfectly safe here," she tried to calm him down, "For one thing, Benza thinks that we are his family and will protect us. Secondly, his senses are far better than ours and he will alert us if danger approaches, and finally, and probably most important, the predators are not interested in us, possibly because we do not act or smell like the other more familiar animals."

As they were a long way from a safe haven, Stef had to take her word about their safety, but every so often he would raise his eyes and nervously scan the vicinity.

The shadows grew long, and they turned for home. Stef shaded his eyes and looked at the sun low on the horizon. Somehow he had expected that it would be white hot, but it was a cooler shade of red, almost orange, and it was far larger than he had expected. His mind tried to recall the old movies that showed the sun, but that was no help, as the suns were all sizes due to photographic and dramatic effects.

"You should not look directly at the sun!" warned Pryme, "It will damage your eyes!"

As Stef turned to look at her, he felt a touch of panic; there was a shadow over his vision so that he could not make out her face. He rubbed his eyes, but the shadow persisted.

"You have temporarily burned out your retina," Ega called out from the shadow, "It will pass in a few moments, but if you stared for a long period at the sun, the blindness would become permanent."

Pryme took his hand and guided him along the path, and after a few minutes, his vision was restored, but he kept a tight hold on Pryme's hand. He looked down at the comparison of their skins; his pale against the golden tones of her hand.

"Has the sun burned your skin to this colour?" He asked, suddenly remembering the papers in Jol's apartment, "I think that it was called a suntan."

"Yes, it was the sun that created my skin colour," Pryme held up their joined hands, "I think that you are starting to tan also, there is a definite pink glow in your skin."

Stef peered at his own arms, but his vision was not quite back to normal and compared to hers, it was still pale. He would look later.

They had the evening meal outside on the rustic table, Ega fetching the food, and Benza waiting patiently for scraps. Stef began to see the attraction of the puppy; it was alert, and the gaping mouth with the drooling tongue gave it a comical appearance if you ignored the prominent canine teeth!

Their discussion was low key, appreciation of the food, certain details about the day's events, such as the waterfall. As they talked, the stars appeared. Stef leant back and watched as they magically appeared, noticing the differences in size and colour.

Pryme touched his arm, "Do you know that the ancients made shapes out of the stars based on the myths and religions?"

"I thought that religion was a myth!" Stef answered, his eyes still fixed on the sky.

"All of those stories meant something important to them in the past," Pryme pointed at a group of stars, "That was always the figure of a man, some said that he was a king, others that he was a warrior, and still others that he was a hunter." Stef looked at where she pointed, but could not make out the shape of anything.

"If we sit here for a while longer, you will see something amazing." Pryme snuggled into his side.

"I never studied anything about the sky," Stef said softly, as though a loud noise would break the vision, "Obviously this is the first time that I have seen the stars. What keeps them up there, and how far away are they?"

"You won't believe it, but they move at incredible speeds, and it is the balance between opposing forces that keeps them there, and as for the distance, it would take many lifetimes to reach the nearest star," Pryme said.

Stef could feel the heat from her body, and her perfume, her natural odour, filled his senses. He knew that he was entering unfamiliar ground, and he was uncertain of what to do. He had liaisons with girls in the City, but these were always recommended by City Control, and only lasted for a few days or a few months. With Pryme, he had a feeling that she would be like her furniture, always there and never vanishing, waiting for his return, something permanent. He had to balance that against the present situation, and that the investigation may put an end to the dream.

Pryme's voice broke into his idle speculation, "It is coming now!" she said softly, and pointed over the top of the mountain.

At first, Stef could see little difference in the star formations, and then he perceived a line of stars gradually emerging from behind the mountain, and as he watched the line crept higher, and behind it followed a solid phalanx of lights and shadows. It stretched right across the sky, a giant slash through eternity! Stef felt the hairs on the nape of his neck stand out, and a clammy hand had seized his heart. He had stopped breathing, but a squeeze from Pryme's hand on his broke the spell.

"What is it?" he gasped.

"That is two galaxies, ours and our nearest neighbour in the cosmos," Pryme answered, "They are in the process of colliding!"

Stef could not take his eyes from the spectacle, "Is that the collision? All of that dust and fire."

"Believe it or not, that dust is what creates stars, not destroy them!" Pryme kept a tight hold of his hand as she explained, "And the fires are the light from stars buried in the dust that illuminate the clouds."

Stef said nothing; he was completely immersed in the majesty of two giants in conflict. It looked like a battle scene in a film he had seen once, frozen in time like a photograph, and in complete silence. The cannons had roared, and the muzzle flames were captured at that moment, and the clouds were the evidence of vast explosions.

"If they are colliding, will there be some damage to us here?" Stef asked.

"To us no, as it will be a long time before the collision really starts, but in our future generations, perhaps a hundred thousand years in the future, there will be radiation, and maybe one of those stars will hit our star," Pryme said that quietly.

"Then everything will be destroyed!" Stef was alarmed, "It seems so random in that we do not know it will happen, just if!"

"But why should we worry at this moment?" Pryme snuggled into his side, "Not very much can be predicted with any accuracy."

Without saying another word, the two watched until the sun faded the stars. Pryme pointed out the various constellations and the stories that went with them. Stef noticed that each collection of stars had more than one story, a different name and that some were linked together in the same story. Once more, Pryme had taken control of the investigation, this time by using the magic of the stars.

CHAPTER ELEVEN

Sleepily, the two ate an early breakfast. Stef felt drained, not by the fact that he had not slept, but by the intake of new experiences and emotions; coming here was a revelation of a world, no, a cosmos that he had never dreamed had existed.

Ega had a new experience for him, strange oval lumps of food. Stef tapped the hard outer surface and wondered how to eat it.

"It is called an egg," Ega explained, "You have to break the shell by tapping it, and then eat the contents."

Stef tapped several times with his knuckle before the shell was broken, and he stared at the milky white content. Pryme had done the same with a spoon and then showed him how to scoop out the soft substance. Stef did the same and found that the flavour was strange but pleasant.

"I understand that at one time it was quite common to eat eggs for breakfast," Pryme said.

"Where do they come from?" Stef asked.

"They are the unborn infants of birds, and sometimes reptiles." Pryme answered, "Rather than develop inside the mother, these are produced, and after a while, the infants emerge."

Stef frowned. The thought of eating unborn children of any creature nauseated him. Pryme noticed his frown.

"They are full of protein and provide energy for the day. Didn't you find it pleasant?"

Stef nodded, "As long as I don't think about what they are!"

"They are easy to find," Ega said, "They lay them in the grass and trees, and the garden drones often bring us a few."

Stef looked out towards the lake and noticed that there were many different birds. They were the source of the food! He compared it to the bland porridge that he usually ate for breakfast, and that made him wonder as to what the bland mash was.

As if reading his mind, Ega brought in two dishes and a steaming pot of something. She ladled out portions into the two dishes. It looked like porridge, similar to that which he had eaten before, but the smell was much more powerful. Tentatively, he took a spoonful. His first impression was spoilt due to the temperature, but when he allowed it to cool, the flavour hit his palate.

"This is real porridge, and comes from the seeds of grasses." Ega told him.

Stef looked at the short green carpet beneath his feet. He was eating grass! In silence, he finished the bowl, his mind whirling with unbidden thoughts.

"That is nothing like the porridge that I have every morning!" he announced as he wiped his mouth on a napkin.

"That is because what you have in the City is not made from natural products!" Ega said, "The bread that you eat here also comes from grass seeds, and if you like, I can prepare other natural foods for you to sample."

"I would not rush into taking samples," Pryme advised, "Your stomach is not used to it, and you could become ill. Take a little now and then, until your body adjusts to it."

"Everything that you eat comes from out there?" Stef said, not believing that it was possible.

Pryme nodded, "At one time, everyone ate natural products!"

"Then what have I been eating all of these years?" he asked in bewilderment.

"Chemicals mainly," Pryme said, "with some yeasts grown in hydroponic farms. A huge quantity can be produced at low cost and quickly in that way, compared to farming natural food, which is labour intensive."

Stef considered that for a moment and realised that eating natural food was an exciting adventure.

"I am going to go for a short walk," Pryme said as she stood, "It aids the digestion. Coming?"

Stef rose with her and felt a strange sensation in his gut. He let out a loud and prolonged burp.

Pryme smiled, "That is one of the effects of natural food, especially if you are not used to it!"

They walked down to the lake. It appeared that this was Pryme's favourite walk, and Stef noticed more details, now that the novelty had worn off. There were flowers on the grass and trees of all shaped, colours and sizes, often accompanied with small insects. The gentle wind moved the grass as though it was liquid, and high above an invisible bird was singing. He felt a sense of joy that he could not explain.

They reached the shoreline and Pryme stepped into the water, and with a swift motion removed the wispy garment. Instead of disappearing to be recycled again, it fluttered on to the sand, and Stef stooped to pick it up, thinking that it had been accidentally removed.

Pryme had carried on walking into the lake until the water reached her waist, then she turned and beckoned Stef to follow.

"I bathe here every morning," she said, "you have no idea how refreshing it feels! Come and join me."

Stef was confused. He held her garment between them, as though it was a shield, and looked at her in astonishment. People did not run around naked, nor did they immerse themselves in water, not that the city possessed pools and lakes that he knew of. He was not embarrassed by her nakedness, just that it was never done.

Seeing his reluctance, Pryme leant backwards, arched her back and fell into the water. For a moment, Stef thought that she had stumbled, but then her head bobbed to the surface, and it was obvious from her smile that she was enjoying herself. Her legs appeared partly out of the water, and Stef realised that she was floating. She kicked her feet and showered him with cold droplets of water.

"You must try it sometime!" she said.

Stef just smiled and contented to watch her splashing around. He noticed that her whole body possessed the same tone; did that mean that she exposed her completely naked body to the sun? Instinctively he looked up and was blinded by the fiery orb. Blinking, he briefly lost sight of everything, and he felt a sense of loss at not watching Pryme playing in the water, however briefly.

Finally, she stepped out of the water. Stef could see the beads of water running down her bronzed skin, following the contours of her body. He had never seen anyone bathe or shower before, and he found the experience disturbing. She stooped over and ran her hands through her hair, shaking and splashing more water on him.

"I will soon dry in the sun," she said and made no attempt to retrieve the garment from him. Instead, she walked along the water's edge, rubbing her hair until most of the water had left the dark strands. Stef followed, admiring the supple movements of her body, and then he remembered the definition that he had found of ancient creatures that lived in the woods and water, nymphs. That was it! Pryme was a nymph of this valley and lake, a wild spirit of nature.

Now he could perceive that the problem he was sent to investigate was Pryme, and how could such a creature exist outside of the rules and conventions of the City. He did not understand how or why the apartment had been created and exposed to the open, which was just a symptom of Pryme herself. He had now to balance that with the question of whether she was doing any harm, and that was much more difficult to answer.

CHAPTER TWELVE

After two days, during which he had eaten several natural foods and seen a lot more of the outside, he returned home. He had forgotten that he had permanently furnished his apartment, and he felt momentarily confused until he remembered. Then it became comfortable in his mind, but he also realised that it was not as comfortable as Pryme's home.

He re-installed the video chart he had been using to solve the problem and then sat in the comfortable armchair. He added a few more notes and sat studying it in silence, but he could not concentrate. He ordered a vase of flowers and then cancelled it when he realised that it would be artificial and lacked scent. Then he ordered a fruit drink, and nearly spat out the first mouthful; it lacked the flavour of Pryme's cordial!

He stood and dismissed the drink. He paced up and down; he felt restless, and what was very obvious, he felt trapped! How could he resolve the problem to the satisfaction of Control? He sat down again and ordered that the window be replaced by a series of pictures of the ancient legends that depicted nymphs, and listened to the murmur of the commentary.

Again he fell asleep! The dream was of Pryme again, and Ega as a young girl and they were both naked, running and dancing through the long grass, the sunlight through the trees dappling their skins. They wore the garlands of wild flowers in their hair, and their laughter was like the chiming of bells. He followed their progress down to the lake where they bathed and swam with the dog Benza. Their laughter was echoed by the cries of the birds swooping above the lake. Stef could not swim, so the spectacle was something new to him, but it appeared natural in the dream.

The call signal roused him, and for a moment he could not recollect where he was. He answered the call and Jol appeared.

"I trust that I have not disturbed you," Jol began, "I have come across another document that I think that you should see."

"What sort of document?" Stef rubbed the sleep from his eyes.

"It is another chart that depicts another phase in the City development." Jol seemed out of breath, "Should I come over to you, or can you come here?"

Stef thought for a second, "I will come over to you!" He had other thoughts on his mind, and Jol may have the answers in his cluttered apartment.

Within minutes, Stef was entering Jol's untidy nest and being greeted by the historian.

"This will be of interest to you," began Jol as he unrolled a large sheet of paper.

Stef bent over the chart, and immediately he noticed something. He jabbed at the sheet with a finger, "What is this?"

Jol's head began bobbing up and down, "I know, I know! It would appear that at one time there were plans to have the outer apartments open, but for some reason, they changed their mind."

"Who changed their mind?" Stef growled. This was not what he had expected!

"Presumably the City Control!" Jol said.

"What would make them change the plans?" Stef frowned. The drawing clearly showed that most of the apartments on the periphery of the City were open to the fields and lake, just as they were with Pryme's apartment, but not one was built. So Pryme's apartment must be a throwback to this project, but why?

"You see these letters here say that these plans were rejected," Jol pointed out a stamp in one corner.

Stef studied the plans closely, observing the neat layout of gardens outside each of the apartments, and here were the trees. Paths crisscrossed the gardens, and he found the one that led to the waterfall.

"This appears to be an outflow from the City," he pointed at the river, "I would also expect that there is an intake somewhere." He dared not reveal that he knew these things long before he had met Jol. The chart did not cover the extent of the lake, and although he searched for the inlet, he could not find it.

"Perhaps it comes from further out, on the other extremities of the lake!" Jol suggested.

Stef grunted. This made the anomaly even more complicated! "Why are these not on City Control's records?"

"Ah! We have an idea about that!" Jol beamed, "Yes we do! We think that at one time all records were manually recorded, perhaps by people, and when that became automated, they simply started again from that point in time."

Stef looked at the librarian in surprise, "That would mean that the earliest phases of the City development are not recorded!"

Jol's head bobbed up and down in agreement, "That is so, and that is why I spend so much time in the archives!"

"Where are these archives?" Stef felt his pulse quicken.

"Not far, in fact just beneath our feet," Jol pointed down at the floor, "We do not need to take the tunnel, as there are some steps. Would you like to see it?"

Stef followed the pointing finger with his eyes. He was aware that parts of the old City were connected by steps and corridors, without any trace of a moving floor, but he had never ventured into the depths before.

He nodded, "But before we go there, do you have any record of the drones, how they were introduced and developed?"

Jol shook his head, "I have not examined that subject, but I think I know someone who has, and with any luck, she will be in the archives!"

The historian led Stef down a corridor, and then two more before descending a flight of steps. Before them was a large door. Jol pressed some buttons and the door slid quietly sideways. Before Stef was a panorama that appeared to be infinite, with rows of shelves under a wide vaulted arch that disappeared into a vague mist. He could discern figures moving in the mist, human figures mostly, but there were a few drones as well.

Stef's jaw dropped, "How big is this?"

"I have never been to the far side," Jol admitted, "All that interests me is on this side."

"Where is this person who studies drones?" Stef frowned, he could spend a lifetime looking for someone in here without success!

"If she is here, it will be in this direction." Jol trotted away without checking if he was being followed. With longer strides, Stef soon caught him up.

"I would have thought that City Control would give you specified tasks!" Stef said.

"Oh no!" Jol shook his head, "We are allowed to follow any subject that we want. City Control has nothing to do with the direction that we explore!"

Stef stopped walking. This was the strangest thing that he had heard! Control is involved in everything! Or so he had been told. Recovering from his surprise, he ran after the historian who had turned off into a side passage.

Jol pointed ahead, "That is her, Mas by name."

Mas turned in surprise at being approached in the archives; it was something unusual. Stef saw a slight figure whose hair was snow white that tumbled over her slim shoulders, and in her hands she held an open file. Stef guessed that she was quite old, but her blue eyes blazed with young curiosity.

"Mas, I am glad that we found you," Jol whispered, "This is Stef who is interested in the drones. That is your area isn't it?"

Mas nodded, and in complete silence beckoned them to follow her, and eventually they arrived at a reading area, some tables and chairs.

"We can talk here," she whispered, "as long as we keep the noise down."

Stef thought that it was ridiculous to whisper, and started in a normal voice, but both Mas and Jol waved their hands for him to lower the volume.

"I would like to know how the drones started!" he whispered.

Mas shrugged, "No one knows, but there are several theories. At one time, long ago, there were no such things as drones, and then some machines were introduced to make other machines. After that, it becomes a confusion as to how the drones came about, but there are stories of things called slaves, by all accounts they were humans that were forced to work, and then we have stories, a few fragments of stories that machines called robots took over the work of the slaves."

Stef was puzzled, "I have never heard of slaves or robots! I can see that drones do all of the manual work and that there may be a connection between them and slaves and robots, but no one instructs the drones, no one forces them!"

Mas nodded, "That is what is puzzling us! There is one fragment, obviously some children's story and absolutely ridiculous, that one slave or robot controlled the world, and even took the human race to the stars!"

Immediately, Stef remembered the night under the stars with Pryme. She was so insistent that he saw the stars, and now Stef wondered why. He began to suspect that the anomaly was not Pryme, her apartment, Ega, or even the dog Benza, it was something totally different!

"Can you show me these fragments of stories?" he asked Mas.

"I can! If you wait here, I'll fetch the file, but what you will do with them is a mystery to me!" Mas said, and walked away.

"I cannot see what you need them for either!" Jol said, "I have seen them, and they must be just stories for the amusement of children."

"Perhaps, but at the very minimum, they provide some background that I lack!" Stef wondered what use they would be, perhaps some insight into ancient times. He was puzzling over the terms slave and robot, and that someone could force others to do something when Mas returned with a memory ball.

"It is all on here," Mas said, placing the ball in Stef's hand, "It contains all of the nonsense stories, but we cannot accept the veracity of them, and they cover a huge area of time. The best of luck to you!"

Back in Jol's apartment, Stef restrained his impatience to see the stories in the memory ball; he wanted a period of quiet contemplation as he studied them. He asked Jol if he could take a copy of the City chart, and was surprised that one copy already existed.

"I was surprised as well," said Jol, "but there were two copies in the archives. I think that there must have been a machine that enabled copies to be made, as it must have been an arduous task to copy them by hand."

Stef stared at him. Did Jol not realise what he had just said? If there were no machines in the past, there would have been a reason, the main reason for slaves and robots!

"Do you have any records about the methods they used to build the City?" he asked the historian.

Jol looked blank, and then shook his head, "No! I do not think that the question has ever arisen. Why would that be important?"

"Just a thought," Stef dismissed the idea, "Thanks for the drawing, and for introducing me to Mas." He picked up the roll of paper and headed for the door, but Jol stopped him.

"If you want documents on the building methods, I could make a search for you." Jol said, "The question has aroused my interest!"

Stef nodded, "If you do not mind. It will just be background knowledge, but welcome just the same, as it will build up a picture of what used to happen in the past!"

CHAPTER THIRTEEN

Back in his apartment, Stef laid out the drawing on the table but found that it wanted to return to its rolled up state as though it had a memory, so he placed the memory ball on one end and ordered a weight for the other end. When it arrived, it was a small ornament of an unknown animal. He thought about that, why had City Control sent him an ornament of an animal! Then he placed that thought at the back of his mind.

He sat in the armchair and looked at Pryme's garden. He was disappointed that they were not there, and he had a sudden urge to leap into the picture and look for them, but that would have been the last of Stef Barak!

Instead, he asked City Control what there was on slaves in the records.

"There is not a great amount, Stef." City Control said, "I can give you some facts and figures if that would suffice!"

Stef was astounded! In a matter of a few days, Control had argued against his choice of viewing, and that had never happened before! For the moment he accepted Control's choice, and a series of views, apparently old artwork showing people doing difficult and strenuous tasks.

Control supplied the commentary as a narrator. "This shows slaves in a place called Egypt in the distant past, and they are building a temple or a tomb out of those large stones they are pulling. Most of the slaves were either not Egyptian, or they were prisoners being punished for some crime."

"What is a temple, or a tomb?" Stef asked, and a picture of a building replaced the toiling slaves.

"This what we refer to as a temple, which can also be a tomb," the narrator said, "The temple is a place of worship to gods, and a tomb was where people were buried once they had died."

"They buried people?" Stef was surprised and horrified, "Why did they not just recycle the person? It seems very wasteful to me!"

"They did not possess the technology at that time to break-down the molecules and return them to the Personnel Vaults as we do, but sometimes they would burn the bodies," the narrator explained, "I agree that it is very wasteful either way, but now we know better!"

"What happened to the slaves?" Stef asked.

"There are a few references to large numbers dying, and some of them were executed at the end of their usefulness," the narrator said, "There does not appear to be a constant pattern as to slavery, except abuse to them all. Eventually, the term slave was changed to worker, with less abuse, and the term worker is also robot in another language, but robots are definitely machines. The word drone is also a synonym for worker."

Stef digested that information before asking another question, "Why did they abuse the slaves and workers?"

"There were various reasons," the narrator said, "The earliest mention was in buildings that were part of their religion. They believed that their god lived in the buildings dedicated to them, and ceremonies were conducted within the buildings by specialised people called priests. Nothing was more important than to please the God, even the fate of the slaves was not that important. Later on the reason was to accumulate vast quantities of wealth."

"How could they force a person to do something against their will?" Stef asked.

"In return for their labours, the slaves and workers were given food and housing, and in a later period, some of the workers were allowed to accumulate a certain amount of wealth for themselves," the narrator answered.

"I have a memory ball here," Stef held up the ball, "Can you please form a reader for me?" A machine appeared with an indentation to receive the ball.

"Thank you Control," Stef said, "I will get back to you with any further questions."

Before viewing the memory ball, Stef ran over all that he had learned. It would appear that all through history, some people had been subjected to enormous abuse and forced to do tasks at the risk of their health and even their very lives, simply for the pleasure of a few. How did that equate with the anomaly of Pryme? Why did she have a drone as a friend? Did Ega build or alter the apartment? Why when he dreamed or viewed them did Ega become a young girl? Did the records in the memory ball have anything to do with the other?

The only way was to view the contents, so Stef dropped the ball into the machine. The first view was of a large, but not very realistic machine. It moved around on smooth surfaces, and it was apparent that there was someone inside making the machine work. The next scene was of something similar, but much smaller, but it still did not resemble a drone. The third scene was of a mechanical man that wore clothes. These were extracts from films, and obviously, the robot figures contained a human being. The final sequence showed a small white figure climbing steps, and that was obviously a machine.

The memory ball supplied an interactive commentary, "These are supposed to be robots, but only the last is a real one. There was a lot of interest in robotics long ago, first as aids in production," The view changed to a production line with mechanical arms performing tasks, "and then the idea developed into prosthetic limbs for injured people," and now the scene was of a man being fitted with an artificial arm. The programmer froze that picture and continued the narration, "The big problem was to create artificial intelligence so that these robots could function autonomously. There was strong resistance to the idea, some saying that we were imitating God, others that robots were roaming freely around would be dangerous. As the range of technology increased, some machines incorporated robotic functions, such as for transport in the air, at sea, and in ground vehicles. Despite a few accidents, the robotic machines were proved to be safer than humans performing the same function, however, when drones appeared they were restricted to working separately from humans. The full autonomous function was never applied to drones."

"So drones and humans do not co-exist in the same room," said Stef, thinking of Ega.

"Exactly! There is a fear that has proved difficult to eradicate within the human population, and one of many other phobias!" The narrator confirmed Stef's statement, and Stef could only just not blurt out a question about Ega. "There are a few stories where laws were invented to prevent a robot from running wild," the narrator added, "these were, the First Law, 'a robot may not injure a human being or, through inaction allow a human being to come to harm'. The Second Law is, 'a robot must obey orders given it by a human being, except when that order would conflict with the First Law'. The Third Law is, 'a robot must protect its own existence, as long as such protection does not conflict with the First and Second Laws'. There is also Zeroth's Law, 'a robot may not injure humanity, or through inaction allow humanity to come to harm'."

Stef frowned, "How can you apply laws to an artificial creature?"

"By applying those laws by manipulating the circuits in what we can refer to as its brain, and artificial brain." The narrator explained, "There is an automatic cut-out that immobilises the robot before any damage is done."

"And drones are robots?" Stef asked.

"Without going into the technicalities, yes in a manner of speaking they are!" the narrator confirmed.

"The creation of laws for robots was to remove the fear of them doing harm," Stef said, "I can see that, but who invented the laws?"

"Again, there is some confusion," the narrator continued, "The old records are very fragmentary, there are mentions of someone called Asimo or Asimov. Perhaps the same person, but one is misspelt, or they could be two different people."

"Why was the City built, and the drones created?" Stef asked.

"To house the human race, and for the drones to perform manual labour, much of which causes harm to a human body." The narrator said.

"So the City and drones were made to create a safe environment for humans?" Stef asked, but he knew the answer.

"That is a perfect way to describe the City!" The narrator sounded pleased.

Stef paused for a moment before asking the next question, but this was directed to Control Central. "What was the anomaly that you sent me to investigate? You were vague about the details!"

"It was something unusual, something unlike anything else in the City," Control said, "As it was unusual, I wanted you to define the amount of deviation, and decide for yourself what should be done."

"Have you followed my investigation?" Stef asked.

"Yes! You have much more to discover before coming to any conclusions." Control replied, "I steered Jol towards you to supply some answers, and Mas will help as well, but the real aid to the inquiries will be Pryme and Ega. At the end of your investigation, you will have to make a decision; it is something that I cannot do!"

For the first time, Control Central had admitted that it was not the all-knowing super-being that everyone believed, and that left Stef in a state of shock. He had also named Ega, and that he must know of her function within the apartment.

"You know of Pryme and Ega, so why did you not inform me at the beginning?" Stef asked.

"I wanted you to form your opinion of them and the situation, and then present your recommendations as to what action should be taken," Control said, "If I had described the situation to you, you would have preconceived ideas and not true ones."

"I have never met anyone like her," Stef said quietly, "She is as free as the air around her, and I cannot see that she, they, are doing anything wrong, although the whole situation contradicts everything that exists in the City."

"Could you live like that?" Control asked.

Stef thought of the two days he had spent in her company, and slowly nodded his head, "It would take a period of adjustment, but I think that it would be possible!"

"From that statement, I suggest that you have not yet fully investigated the situation and identified the anomaly!" said Control.

CHAPTER FOURTEEN

In the days that followed, Stef had still not fully recovered from the surprise statement from Control Central. For all of known history, Control had steered humanity to its present state, but now a decision had been handed over to a mere mortal, aided by historians, a wild nature-loving woman, and her drone servant and dog! What was worse for Stef was that he had still not defined the question!

He wrestled with the problem without any satisfactory result. In the process, he gathered many notes that did not appear to lead anywhere, so eventually, he sought out Jol again.

The chubby face of the historian looked surprised to see Stef. One reason was that Stef had physically travelled to the apartment without first informing Jol of his intention.

"What can I do for you?" Jol looked odd, and Stef realised that he was wearing some old-fashioned spectacles. Some people did rather than have the medrone correct their vision.

"I'm sorry to invade your privacy, but I wanted to spend some time talking to you and the other historians," Stef explained.

"You are most welcome!" Jol said, "If I can be of any assistance, but I do not see how."

"That's the problem!" Stef sighed, "If I explain what has happened, do you promise not to breathe a word to anyone else, or make a record of it until I say so?"

Jol's eyes became round in surprise, and made larger by the magnification of the lens, "Of course you can say what you want, and I will not say a word! Is this something to do with being on the Outside?"

Stef nodded, "It is, but I want to put it into context!"

"That is important!" Jol agreed nodding.

Stef then started telling Jol about being sent by Control Central to sort out the anomaly, and that the nature of the anomaly had not been cited, and as he described Pryme's apartment and Pryme, Ega, the other drones, and the garden and lake. Jol's face reflected his amazement, but he did not interrupt once.

"That is it!" Stef finished, "Control wants me to identify the anomaly, and then make recommendations. For all of her peculiarities and her situation, I cannot see that Pryme is doing anything illegal in any sense, even though it is irregular and different to anyone else."

Jol said nothing, just sat on a stool and nodding. He was running the story through his mind.

"First I have to identify the anomaly," Stef continued, "and Control has intimated that I had not done so! What is more, I have to correct the anomaly, as Control Central cannot! That was the biggest surprise of all!"

Jol finally stirred himself, "She is a throw-back, Pryme, living as people did in the past, but that is not necessarily wrong! I can see now why Control sent me to meet you; this has something to do with the past," and then after a short pause, "and to the future!"

Stef had an idea, "Would you live in the Outside?"

Jol looked horrified at the thought, "No! I have a fear of open spaces, even the expanse of the archives disturb me, and that is why I prefer to work here."

"I wondered if you would meet Pryme," seeing the increased distress on Jol's face, Stef hurriedly added, "You would not need to go beyond the apartment, but I would be interested in your observations."

A sudden sheen of sweat had formed on Jol's brow, and he licked his lips nervously, "For the sake of the investigation, I would try to endure it, but it may be better if we visited in the normal way." He was referring to visi-meeting.

Stef stopped talking in surprise. Why had he not thought of that? Was it because he was so taken up with the Outside. Perhaps he wanted someone else's impressions. He realised that Pryme and the Outside were becoming an obsession. Or was it just Pryme that was the obsession?

"Of course we can," Stef calmed the historian, "I will set it up right now!"

"Give me a moment or so," flustered Jol, wiping his face on his sleeve, "I would like some refreshment first. Oh, that was a moment!" He ordered some hot beverage for both of them and sat nervously sipping at the drink. Gradually the colour was restored to his face, and he smiled apologetically at Stef.

Stef intercepted Jol's apology, "I know how you must feel. When she first took me Outside, I was about to run away!"

"Oh, it is much worse than that!" Jol said, "I can feel my heart almost stop beating just at the thought!"

"If you are prepared, I'll make contact with Pryme!" Stef said, and Jol nodded quickly.

It was Ega's pleasant voice that greeted them, "How nice to see you again Stef, and you have a friend."

"Hello Ega, we wish to talk to Pryme, if she is available," Stef said.

"She is in the garden, but I have sent Benza to fetch her," Ega said, "She will be disappointed that you did not come here."

"Benza can talk?" Stef said. If the answer had been to the affirmative, he would not have been surprised!

Ega gave one of her tinkling laughs, so reminiscent of her mistress's laugh, "Not in the way that you mean, but she can convey a message that the mistress is required here. They will not be very long."

Just as she finished speaking, Benza came bounding into the room, and Pryme followed shortly, panting at the effort of keeping up with the dog.

Stef kept an eye on Jol and noticed that he was at first taking in the décor of the room, as well as Ega, until Benza and Pryme arrived, and then his jaw dropped in surprise.

"Hello Stef, and I see that you have a friend with you!" Pryme said after regaining her breath.

"This is Jol," Stef placed his hand on Jol's shoulder, "He is a historian who is helping me."

"Hello Jol! Has he coerced you into solving the problem of me?" Pryme smiled as she spoke. She flung herself on the sofa, dressed in her usual scanty garment.

"H-hello!" Jol stuttered, "There was no coercion needed, it is a fascinating subject in its own right!"

"I am a fascinating subject!" Pryme laughed and threw her head back.

"I-I am sure that you are," Jol kept stammering, "but I was referring to the conundrum that Control has set us!"

"So now I am a conundrum!" Pryme set off on another long peal of laughter, waving her hands to indicate that they should change the subject.

Jol willing changed subject, "Is that a real dog?" he asked.

Pryme's laughter subsided, and she called Benza, who came over to have his ears rubbed. "This is a genuine dog and a very dear friend!" she stated.

"You have some strange friends!" Jol said.

"And you don't?" Pryme answered, "All of those strange fellows burrowing away in the archives!"

"Y-yes, we are an odd sort, but we are all human!" Jol said. Stef wondered how she knew of the archives.

"If you can separate humans from dogs successfully, I will agree!" Pryme said, "I find that dogs are much better companions than most humans!"

"I was also referring to the drones!" Jol replied, "Surely they are not human or dog!"

"You will have to take that up with Ega," Pryme allowed Benza to climb on to the sofa, "I am not so sure that you would win the argument!"

"Are all of these items manufactured and not replicated?" Jol returned his attention to the room.

Ega answered him, "Every single thing here was made by drones, chiefly myself!"

"From materials out there, in the Open?" Jol gestured furtively towards the windows, "I take it that is the real Outside and not just another replica?"

"You saw the mistress and Benza come in from there," Ega pointed out, "so it must be real, and yes, all of the materials came from the Outside!"

"I was not fully believing Stef when he told me this," Jol turned to Stef, "I apologies for doubting you, but this is incredible!"

"When will you grace us with a visit?" Pryme asked.

Jol coughed, "I regret to say that I rarely travel, and I have a fear of the Open!"

"I have heard that all fear is irrational!" Pryme said.

"I have heard the same, but it is there none-the–less!" Jol glanced briefly at the blowing material over the windows.

"We will see Stef again!" Pryme stated, drawing her knees up to her chin and gazing at Stef.

"Of course you will," he replied, "There is still a lot to sort out!"

The connection broke, and Jol did not move from the stool. Stef studied him as they both thought about the meeting. Finally, Jol turned to Stef and raised a finger.

"Thank you for introducing me to Pryme," he said, "but I have to go back through the records to check a few things before I can make a comment, except that it was enlightening!"

"Well now you have seen it with your own eyes, and you know that the situation exists!" Stef said.

"Yes indeed!" Jol nodded and made his cheeks wobble, "Without seeing it, I would never have taken your description seriously, but you also did not see what I saw, and that is what I must check on. That drone, Ega was most interesting!"

Stef was surprised at Jol's words! They had been looking at the same room, so surely they saw the same scene, or was Jol referring to things in a different way?

CHAPTER FIFTEEN

Jol's mind was in a whirl. Stef had left him deep in thought; it was true that Jol had seen a lot more than he had indicated, and it was that which enabled him to put aside his nervousness at seeing glimpses of the Outside through the moving curtains. Yes, that was the word he recalled from some scrap of history, curtains.

He cleared his mind and thought of the encounter. Pryme was as carefree as Stef had said, even more so, and the drone was surprising; he had never heard a drone speak for so long before, and that made him wonder about the discussion they could have had about the nature of drones. And then there was the dog! He remembered that another name for a dog was hound and that they could be vicious animals and had been banned long ago, but Benza appeared to be friendly and docile.

The drone Ega, on the other hand, was remarkable; it had perfected various methods of manufacturing and acted as one of the household servants he had seen in old movies. She also supplied technical knowledge far beyond the normal level of drones, and she talked incessantly.

Then there was the apartment: being open to the Outside was a plan that was abandoned early in the development of the City, but here it pops up unannounced! There was Pryme's choice of furnishings, or was it Ega's? A simple request would provide any article in a moment, but here the materials were carefully chosen, and then time is taken to shape them. Jol had no idea how long it would take to make a chair or a table, but it was presumably some days, and when finished, it was kept and cherished.

All of this pointed back to the times when the travellers in the open vehicle had lived. The question was, 'why is their attention being directed to an archaic way of life?' That stumped Jol, and he spent several hours walking back and forth in his apartment, occasionally stopping and pulling out a document. He pinned up the two charts showing the early development of the city, unaware that this action was also archaic.

Without consciously knowing, his feet took him to the archives where he stood in deep thought for some time, and then he started walking until he suddenly realised where he was. Myopically he blinked and tried to get his bearings, and failed; he had never ventured into this section of the vaults before. However, he was recognised, and a hand touched his elbow.

"You look lost Jol!" said a quiet voice. On turning, Jol found the keen eyes of an old friend seriously studying him.

"Yes I am! Hello Sak!" Jol sounded flustered, "I was thinking through a problem in my apartment, and then I found myself here, wherever here is!"

"You're in my section," said Sak, "Was the problem anything to do with machinery?"

"No –no, at least I don't think so!" Jol shook his jowls. Was it about machinery?

"Well, what was the last thing that you remember thinking about?" Sak said helpfully.

"Um, er, it was about the beginnings of the City," Jol recalled his earlier thoughts.

"They used machines then before there were drones. Does that help?" Sak had continued to hold his friend's elbow, afraid that something would happen to Jol.

Jol slowly shook his head, "No! At least I do not think so; it was about the transport, the tunnels!" He placed a finger on his lower lip.

"The tunnels!" Sak looked surprised, "No wonder you're confused, the tunnels came after the City was created. I thought everyone knew that!"

"Oh no, not the tunnels, I mean the ancient way of transport systems they had before the City that they called roads." Jol corrected him.

"Not my field I'm afraid," Sak pulled a face, "It does not seem interesting to me, not attractive at all! You need to see Ree; I think that he has an interest in that sort of thing. Follow me, and we'll track him down."

Ree turned out to be the youngest historian that Jol had ever met. His hair stood out from his head in a dark, unkempt mop.

"Old transport systems! Wonderful contraptions!" Ree said enthusiastically when the subject of Jol's visit was explained. Sak left them to their conversation.

"I was interested in their road systems specifically," Jol said.

"All of the systems were interlinked in some way or other, and at different times!" Ree explained, "To understand them, you have to start at the earliest times and follow through the evolution!"

"Oh dear!" Jol frowned, "I hope that it does not take too long!"

"No problem! There is not a lot to find!" Ree shook his head, "What I can tell you will not take very long.

At some time, so long ago that we cannot put a date on it, there were no vehicles, and then someone invented the wheel!"

"I always imagined that there were always vehicles!" Jol looked astonished.

"It was a very, very long time ago," Ree said, "Very long! Then they adapted a number of vehicles to be pulled by animals. Then they invented a combustion engine to replace the animals, and these were fitted in a variety of machines, those that went on water, some on the roads, others on the railways, and finally in flying machines. Some of those flew to the stars!"

Jol's jaw dropped open, "The stars!" he whispered. He was uncomfortable in large rooms, and the thought of the Outside made him tremble, but travelling through space, a featureless nothing made him almost swoon!

"If you come back to my apartment, I can show you pictures of most of the vehicles and these engines," Ree suggested.

"Are these on record?" Jol gulped out his question.

"Not many!" Ree said, "I found most of them in a huge disordered file, as though no one bothered with them."

"Then I will accompany you to your apartment if it is not too much to ask," Jol said, and they made their way to Ree's apartment.

The pictures of automobiles, and some larger vehicles called trucks, Jol was familiar with, but the ships and aircraft were totally new to him, although he realised on a closer inspection that he had seen parts of them in the background of other photographs without Realising what they were.

"These went to the stars?" he whispered in awe.

Ree laughed, "These did not have the performance to do that! This is what they flew to the stars in!" With a flourish, he revealed a large photograph of some machine spewing out clouds of smoke and flame. To Jol, it looked terrifying, as though the machine was in the process of destruction!

"That is called a rocket!" Ree explained, "It uses a different type of combustion engine that burns fuel at a tremendous rate; most of the machine is a fuel tank!"

"Dear me! It looks very powerful!" was all that Jol could say.

"They stopped using them, and the other combustion engines after a very short time. It was because there was a shortage of the fuel, and they went on to other methods that I have yet to find." Ree said, holding the picture up with an expression of pride.

"That is very impressive, but I was wondering about the roads; was there a system for crossing over water, deserts, and mountains?" Jol tore his eyes away from the picture and looked around the room.

"Oh yeah!" Ree reluctantly rolled the picture up, "All roads were numbered, and there were tunnels and bridges across rivers, but over large quantities of water, they had to use the ships to carry the automobiles. I have a picture of that happening!" He searched through some paper rolls and brought out a picture of automobiles entering the cavernous jaws of a ship. To Jol, it looked as though the ship was devouring them!

"Then how did the roads that we have now come into existence, the tunnels?" Jol asked.

Ree shrugged, "I don't know! It appeared to happen just as the City was starting to be built, or not long after, and it was a bit chaotic then, so the records, if there were any, have been lost for a long time. I do not know how they work, and so I cannot trace a connection to the earlier transport."

"Could you place any of this on a memory ball, so that I can study it in leisure?" Jol asked, "And do you know how they built these ancient roads and bridges. Perhaps the machines themselves also may show some light on my research."

"I can do that today!" Ree confirmed, "I will send you everything that I have if you think that it will help!"

"We shall see!" Jol said, "Would any of these vehicles be used in the road construction? That would also be of some assistance. When did the tunnels first appear?"

"I'll look it up! Your research is starting to interest me!" Ree said, "Please keep me informed of your progress."

CHAPTER SIXTEEN

"This is all very interesting, but how can it help us?" Stef stared at the screen in Jol's apartment as picture after picture slowly cycled through.

"You want to know how the City started, and I have found out that when that occurred, they were using machines like this to build the City, and without a drone in sight!" Jol replied and pointed to the obviously human figures.

Stef killed the retort that had started to form on his lips. Jol's last remark about drones was well timed, as a series of pictures appeared showing men, and some women, performing hard tasks, such as felling trees, building roads and structures; things that are now undertaken by drones. How did that fit into the picture that had started to form in his mind?

People appeared to spend most of their time in the Outside, exposed to the weather and other hardships. Now it also seemed that they performed manual tasks while they were outside. One picture made him blink; it showed a group of men walking on steel beams high above a city, and so much at ease that they sat there and ate their lunch! Stef could not imagine anyone that he knew that could perform such feats!

A phrase crept into his mind, something that he had read many years ago; 'In these days there were giants!' People were stronger and hardier then than people of today. He tried to imagine what it would be like to walk on steel beams high in the air or to physically move rocks and soil from the ground. He gave up trying to put himself in their place!

As though reading his mind, Jol said, "It was different then, a different philosophy and way of life!" Stef just grunted in reply.

Now a series of scenes appeared on the screen showing some manufacturing process, and this time there were many women standing at machines, and from those machines, rolls of cloth were produced, and then another scene showing women working on what Stef thought was an aircraft, their hands and faces smeared with some dark substance. And they seemed happy! It certainly was a different way of life!

"I suspect that the City was started in this fashion, and then at some time the drones and our tunnels appeared," Jol said.

"I wonder if they suffered through doing these tasks!" Stef wondered.

"Oh yes!" Jol gave a command and the scene changed to a view of a man with his legs partially damaged and others obviously about to do something. That something was evident on the next picture that showed another man with no legs. Stef winced!

"Barbaric!" he exclaimed, "Couldn't they provide new legs, or rebuild his own legs?" He was answered with another photograph of a man standing on crude steel supports.

"Obviously not at that time!" Jol said, "I collected from another historian some data on the Medicare available then, and they could do virtually nothing in most cases. I have some data that indicates that they were developing a regrowth system against damage and disease, and strangely enough, some people objected to the development program."

Stef whirled onto the historian, "Why? They would prefer to see people suffer for the rest of their lives?" he was wondering if everything in the past was so barbaric!

"Ah! There is something about that," Jol looked uncomfortable, "The average life was about seventy or eighty years, and most of these cases occurred during twenty to fifty range, but some exceptional cases lived to just over one hundred years. You could say that they lived in this state for only half of their lives!"

Stef gaped at Jol, "Only eighty years! I am twice that now and considered to be just approaching my best years! What a dismal existence they had!"

"Undoubtedly living Outside and performing these strenuous tasks took their toll on the human body, and that gives us a reason for the emergence of the drones," Jol said.

Then Stef thought of Pryme, "But they also enjoyed the Outside, and possibly most of the hard work! There is a puzzle here that needs solving along with the other!"

"I think that we can safely assume that the City and drones were created to protect us, or at least for our benefit!" Jol said.

"Protect us against what?" Stef asked, "From what I have seen of the Outside, there is not very much there to injure us, and we certainly do not have to work as they did. Is there something I have not seen?"

"How long have you spent outside?" Jol asked.

"Just a few days, but I did not suffer!" Stef answered defensively.

"Are you sure that nothing occurred that caused just a temporary discomfort?" Jol looked enquiringly at his companion.

Stef was just about to deny such an event when he remembered how looking at the sun had affected his vision.

"Aha!" Jol saw the hesitation, "What was it?"

"I looked at the sun, and for a few minutes I was blinded, but it was nothing to cause concern in the long run!" Stef thought of the cold water of the rain and lake, and then that he had passed out when seeing the stars for the first time.

"There was more!" Jol pointed an accusing finger, "I can see it on your face!"

Stef slowly nodded, "I saw the stars for the first time, and I fainted, and the weather can be uncomfortable."

"Interesting!" Jol murmured, "A physical discomfort and a severe psychological discomfort, but did you see the stars again?"

"Yeah, and there were no problems!" Stef said softly as the memory pleasantly returned, "We stayed all night looking at the stars and talking."

"You enjoyed it!" Jol said triumphantly, "No doubt due to your companion as well!" Jol's smile developed into a gentle laugh.

For the first time in his life, Stef felt the blood tingling through his face. He blushed!

"It would appear that the pleasures outweigh the discomforts and dangers!" Jol continued, "There is the answer to that riddle!"

"But that still leaves the question of why build the City to protect us!" Stef recovered his composure, "I saw nothing that would cause that reaction!"

"Nothing that you recognised!" Jol looked pointedly at Stef, "I think that you should return to Pryme and question yourself about every single thing that you see and experience. Her drone Ega would probably know more!"

CHAPTER SEVENTEEN

Stef did not immediately take up Jol's suggestion. He took the memory ball and studied for more details. He had become accustomed to his apartment, now permanently decorated with furniture and decorations, although still reproductions and not real as at Pryme's. Now he sat in his comfortable armchair, drinking from his cups and glasses, and ate from his table. True, he still used the recycler to provide food and provide clean plates, but he felt a sense of belonging that he had never experienced before, and then recalling Jol's advice, he tried to analyses the sensation. His only conclusion was that it was a feeling of comfort.

He ran through all of the research material slowly, taking each piece and giving it due consideration. There was a whole section on wars through many generations. Stef did not know when there had been a war, certainly not recently, and he was confused; there was a scene where men were loading something into an aircraft, but he could not make out if it were fuel or a weapon. Then there was another scene where men were advancing over mud, and then falling down; were they injured? At the end of the sequence, he had found no reason why they had a war, and that was the most senseless thing of all!

One photograph had Stef puzzled until he realised that it was of bodies stacked up in piles, impossibly thin bodies with their eyes sunk in dark pits. He felt a shudder of horror as he viewed this; was this result of some military action, but he could not relate the weapons he had seen with the result of mass starvation.

The last photograph was of a ship firing something like rockets, all flame and smoke. He let it remain there while he thought through what he had seen. Clearly, there had been many wars, but no reason was given for hostility. All of these wars were at the time of the beginning of the City or earlier, so what had changed? Why had there been no wars since then? Or had there been a war that was not recorded in any way? He was suspicious of Control not recording everything!

It was some time before he moved on to the next subject, the sight of men and women dying in thousands had depressed him, and the numbers and different types of weapons made available to end life was shocking, he was not even sure if what he had seen was weapons and what were the result of their use.

The next subject was industrial machinery, some in manufacturing, but the largest were outside, the main purpose being to remove tons of soil. Why they were doing this was again beyond his imagination; men standing dwarfed by the machines beside them, and in turn, the machines were dwarfed by an enormous excavation. Were they building or taking something? He could see a vague link between these monstrous machines and the mass destruction of people.

He called up Jol and posed a question, "Where do you get all of these unrecorded documents?"

Jol looked surprised, "There is a huge area in a part of the archives that has many documents, photographs, and that sort of thing. We have to search through all of it to find anything of interest."

Stef leapt at the statement, "Are you telling me that there is a huge amount of data that City Control has no idea about?"

"I don't know if Control is aware of the data or not, the question has never come up," Jol wiped his head with one hand, "We assume that this was the remaining data that was previously recorded by humans, and just left when the drones took over!"

"What do you mean by 'take over'?" Stef asked.

Jol thought for a moment. Obviously, this was something he had learned long ago and partially forgotten, then he remembered, "There was an edict by the Council that all humans should hand over their tasks to the drones, and then follow a life of ease. This was followed by another edict that allowed those that wanted to choose a task that they found interesting. I think that I remember that there were some problems with discontent among the humans that caused the second edict. As you can see, I chose to be a historian!" He said the last lightly, happily.

"Have you seen either edict?" Stef asked.

Jol shook his jowls, "I cannot even remember where I heard it!"

"Thank you Jol!" Stef said, "I would like to see this mountain of data sometime, just out of curiosity!"

Jol nodded, sending his jowls wobbling in a different direction, "Any time that you want, but I cannot see how it would help you!"

"Just background!" Stef said, "There seems to be more background then facts! Until next time!"

If what Jol had said was true, then there could be unrecorded data concerning events after building the

City had commenced. He turned back to the picture of the ship that was firing rockets. Most of these wars were with the aid of machines, but machines had taken over the running of the City, and since then there had been no wars on record. Control kept the records, and Stef had seen how that could be manipulated, so what was the truth?

Despite the realisation that Control Central may not supply a correct answer, Stef made contact.

"Yes Stef, how can I help you?" Control asked.

Stef was unsure of the question, and for a few moments he waved his hands and tried to form words. Finally, he managed to do so.

"I have been looking at the lives and machines before the City was built, and to me, it is simply confusion!"

"I have noticed your research," Control answered, "I agree that it was a confusing time, and for many reasons. One thing that you must accept is that humans have a propensity to ignore the truth! Many of the wars that you have viewed were the result of political lies and an inbuilt xenophobia. Eradicating that has been the most difficult of tasks!"

"That makes no sense to me!" Stef said and frowned, "If the truth is ignored, or it is manipulated, there will be incorrect solutions to problems! Who would lie?"

"Ah, there you are beginning to understand the confusion and conflict in the days before the City." Control answered, "The world was divided into different parts, each being governed by a group of humans or even a single person, but there were always factions that disagreed with the government, sometimes violently!"

Stef took a gamble, "Why is little or none of this in the records?"

Control gave a small chuckle, "Jol was correct when he said that the drones took over manual work and that much of the material during the transition was never placed in the archives."

"But you have just related the way the world used to be run, and that means that there are records!" Stef pointed out.

"I am much more than the recorder of events!" Control said enigmatically.

"Then why are these records not available?" Stef demanded an answer.

"Perhaps they are of little use in today's society," Control sounded amused, "With the drones, there is little need for giant machines, conflicts, or personal artefacts!"

"What were the machines taking from the ground?" Asked Stef.

"Various things!" replied Control, "Mostly it was raw materials to make metals that would be processed, and eventually objects would be manufactured. Sometimes they buried things!"

"So why were the drones and City created?" Stef held his breath.

"The creation of the City that is run by the drones was to remove the need for thoughtless destruction, including conflicts," Control said, "By removing the sources of greed and argument, the safety of humans was ensured. However, that is changing."

"Changing! How?" Stef felt alarmed at those words.

"The answer is with Pryme and Ega," Control said, "Try not to see the obvious, and extend your thinking beyond today!"

CHAPTER EIGHTEEN

Control's conversation did not help Stef at all! There was a continued reference to something else, something further than he had gone, but there was also a reference to something obvious. Was it something that Stef had already seen, but dismissed as nothing to do with the problem? Having said that, the problem had still to be recognised as well!

He dithered and wasted time, putting off the inevitable visit to Pryme. He found that while he was with her the investigation drifted into other areas at her instigation, and Stef found that he had other questions that had nothing to do with the investigation. He went with Jol down to the 'raw' archives, huge mounds of paper that stretched for miles in air-conditioned chambers. He did notice that drones were working on the initial collecting of the material. Presumably, historians would pick through that to find something of their interest.

Stef did not pass any comments, none worthwhile mentioning, but he thought that it was a haphazard way to achieve a result. A pile of data could sit for a lifetime or more before a historian would stumble on what he was seeking. Compared to the rest of the City's well-ordered activities, this was a shambles! He made a mental note to say something to Control about this waste of time and energy.

Finally, he could not put off the inevitable, and he dressed in the clothes that Ega had made and embarked on the long journey to Section AO356-12-54992. He had time to think as the bubble travelled along the endless tunnel. What did Section AO356-12-54992 mean? He summoned up a list of sections and read them on the visor screen; some were obviously a lot higher than Pryme's, up to fifteen digits on the first part alone, but what did the numbers signify?

This time he arrived early but after breakfast. At least he would not be distracted by tasting new foods! Pryme answered the door, with Benza forcing his way past her to sniff at the visitor, his tail wagging with recognition.

"Welcome Stef!" Pryme said with a beaming smile. As usual, she was dressed in a flimsy garment.

"I hope that you don't mind my company for a while?" Stef managed to bend down and pat Benza's head; his earlier revulsion had disappeared, and the dog seemed happy to be patted, "There is quite a bit more for me to understand!"

"You are welcome anytime!" Pryme's eyes shone like searchlights, illuminating everything that she looked at, and at the moment she was staring at Stef, and he felt his heart swell.

"We are sitting outside!" Pryme led him to where Ega was standing by the rough table.

"Would you like some refreshment Stef?" Ega asked. Forgetting his resolve, Stef nodded, and within moments he was tasting another strange flavour.

Pryme placed a golden hand on his knee, "Now Stef, you must tell us how we can help you!"

Stef looked down at the hand and then at Ega, and an idea began to form in his head, "I will tell you of what I have seen, and some of the facts I have found. First of all, there was a time when the City or drones did not exist, all of the work was carried out by humans, and sometimes unwillingly. Before the City there were a number of towns that were connected by a series of roads, but not roads as we know them; those roads and the towns were exposed to the open air, just as you are now. People enjoyed working and travelling in the open! Then they started to build the City. Why this was done is unknown, although everything mentions that it was to protect us, but from what?"

He paused and took a sip of the fruity drink, and Pryme leant forward, "You do like sitting here under the sky, don't you?"

"I have become accustomed to it," Stef agreed, "but some of my associates are terrified at the thought!"

"But there is nothing to be afraid of!" Pryme raised her arms to the skies, "Nothing has harmed us since we lived here!"

"I know, but that does not mean that something will not happen in the future," Stef nodded, "but I do not think that what was on the minds of those who instigated the City."

Pryme looked surprised, "What could be dangerous here?" She looked out over the garden, and a tiny crease appeared between her eyes.

"That may give us an insight into what it is that I am supposed to investigate," Stef said, "but there is something else that occurred to me on the way here. This is called the City and I found that there are more addresses than could be housed under this mountain." He pointed over the roof of Pryme's apartment to where the mountain soared and where water froze. Both Pryme and Ega followed his finger and stared up to the snowy summit.

Stef continued, "There is also the question of the length of time to get here. It is a very long journey and at very high speed, during which time I could have travelled under many mountains."

It was Ega who realised what he was saying, "You travelled from another City!"

"That is my conclusion," Stef agreed, "but why do we only refer to one city, the City, why not First City and Second City, or as many as there are?" He looked from one to the other, but it was obvious that there was no answer forthcoming.

He leant forward to emphasise his words, "When this City was started it was with human workers, plus some heavy machinery. Then it was open to the skies, every apartment like yours with a garden, until the drones appeared and everyone went underground. Why?"

"Now I am feeling scared!" Pryme drew her knees up and hugged them.

"Why?" Stef leant forward, "This is almost as you live now!"

"I don't want to know the reason why, it just feels right without asking questions!" Pryme's expression as she looked into his eyes was one of pleading to go no further.

Stef relented, "It may not be as terrible as you think!"

Pryme shook her head, "I don't want this to change, Ega and I are happy as things are, and we don't need reasons!"

Stef looked at Ega. The drone had not moved or uttered a word since he had started to relate his findings, and the face showed no expression to reveal her feelings, its feelings he reminded himself, it was just a drone! "Are you happy Ega?" he asked.

"I am content as far as I can be!" Ega answered, "I am not sure what happiness is."

He would not have expected more from a drone, and Ega's reply was still more than he would have expected; how can a drone be content? Why did Pryme not want things to change? What was the danger that humans feared in the past? Is that danger relevant now?

CHAPTER NINETEEN

Stef backed off from further questions, contenting himself with just observations. Pryme reacted to that in her usual carefree manner. She asked Ega to fetch some cookies, and then picked up an object from the ground and teased Benza, until finally she threw it down the garden and the dog ran off to find it. It was as though Stef had never raised the questions!

While Pryme played with the dog, Stef turned his attention to Ega. He had the idea that she/it knew more than she said, but it would not be easy to tease the words from her.

"What do you think of the questions I posed?" he asked her.

"The questions cover a wide area," Ega stood facing him, showing that he had her full attention, "From what I have learned, the drones came well after the City building commenced, and as to why the City was built, I have very little idea at all. I am not aware of any danger from the Outside."

"You forgot to include why this apartment is the only one exposed to the Outside," Stef said. Out of all of the questions, this was the one that he thought Ega would know the answer to, and try hard not to reveal.

Ega threw up her arms in a very human gesture, "I have no idea! It was just like this when we arrived. If anyone has the answer, it is Control!"

Stef was not put off, "Why did you start making things?"

"It was to please the mistress." Ega replied, "She saw in old movies that people kept their furnishings, even valuing them highly, and she hated waking every day to a bare apartment."

"You're very accomplished!" Stef said, "Why are you attached to Pryme, and when did that start?"

For the first time, Ega paused before answering, and then, "From the time she was born! I was one of the fostdrones. It was recognised that her brain pattern did not fit into any of the educational sectors, so I was to accompany her at all times until it was deemed that she had found her purpose."

"So she was removed from the nursery!" At last, some of the answers were appearing! As all babies are taken to the nursery as soon after birth as possible, and there they are tended by drones, fostdrones, and they are steered in the direction that her natural abilities took her before formal education in that subject. Obviously, she did not fit into the preconceived slots for formal education. He had heard of such things, not often, but they were cared for by the City – by Control! The devious old devil had known about her all along, but she could not be the anomaly in question, as Control could easily have solved that at the time.

It also solved the problem of Ega, why she was a friend/servant to Pryme, and why she did what she did. Was it an attempt to find a slot in today's society for her mistress? That also explained why there were no previous records, but it did not explain the apartment.

Pryme threw the dog toy towards them, bringing both her and the dog back to them, panting and sweating.

"I feel like a swim!" Pryme said, "And so does Benza! Promise that you will at least step into the water this time." She laughed teasingly at Stef. "You would feel invigorated by splashing around in the cool lake!"

Stef smiled, "I'll walk with you, but I don't promise anything. Can Ega join us?" Now that he understood the nature of the friendship between human and drone, his observations would be more accurate.

"Let us have a picnic!" Pryme called out, "Ega, be a sweet and fetch a basket for the picnic!"

So they walked down to the lake shore. Stef noticed different birds now, fluttering in the trees and making shrill calls. As soon as they arrived, Pryme threw off her garment and dived into the water, with Benza joining her in obvious delight to both. Stef sat down and watched, and for the first time, Ega sat next to him. The normal protocol for drones in the presence of humans was to stand and wait for orders, but this was not a normal drone.

"Why don't you join them?" Ega asked.

"For one, I cannot swim!" Stef answered, "In fact, I have never entered a body of water in my life!"

"Are you scared?" the drone asked.

"Probably! Fear of the unknown is very common." He smiled ruefully.

"So it was with the mistress when we first arrived," Ega informed him, "We had no idea that the apartment was open to the Outside, and she stood in the window for hours, trying to overcome her fears, and then one day she just stepped into the garden. When it first rained, she screamed and ran inside, and as for the thunder and lightning! Over time, she conquered her fears, or at least most of them."

119

"She still fears some things then?" he observed. He then on an impulse, he stood and strode down to the water, kicked off his shoes and carried on walking until the water was up to his waist, and he was face to face with a surprised Pryme.

"Well done!" she exclaimed, "But the effect is better without clothes!"

Stef pulled the shirt off and threw it towards the shore, then he removed the sodden trousers and threw them after the shirt.

"Is that better?" The sensation was like being in a shower, a cold shower, but more intense. He could feel the movement of water as it encircled his legs, and under his feet, he could feel the sand shifting under his weight.

"Tell me! Does it feel better?" Pryme rose out of the water and with a laugh, violently pushed him. In an instant, he had lost his footing on the shifting sand and found he was completely immersed in the lake. In a panic, he thrashed around until he found the lake bed again and stood up, just as Ega had grasped his arm. She had stepped into the water to save him!

Water was pouring out of his nose and mouth as he bent over gasping for air. On his other side stood Pryme with her hands over her mouth and her eyes wide in horror. She was saying something, but all he could hear was a distant murmur as his ears were still filled with water. At last, he could make sense of her words.

"Oh, Stef, I am sorry! I forgot that you had never been in water before. Please forgive me!"

Stef coughed out the last of the water, "Of course I forgive you, but it was also a useful experience. Just don't do it again!"

Ega tugged at his arm, "Come and sit down. It must have been a shock. You can dry in the sun in a few minutes."

Stef allowed himself to be led away from the water by the woman and the drone, and he lay down under the sun, his eyes closed as he thought about the experience. This was another danger that he should record for Jol. When Pryme and the dog were playing in the water, sparkling drops flung in the air, it looked like fun, but it held a dangerous secret.

As though reading his mind, Ega spoke up, "The Sea used to be called the Widow Maker, as so many men have lost their lives in her depths. It has remained a mysterious force since the dawn of time, but attracted men on to her because of that mystery."

Stef opened one eye and gazed at the drone, "Do you have any more information about water that I should know?"

"Lots! It is the source of all life!" the drone said, "Without water, life could not exist, at least not as we know it. The majority of creatures alive today are water creatures, mostly small, but there are larger species." She/it patted his chest, "You had better turn over or the sun will burn you."

"How did you learn so much?" Stef obligingly turned over, and as he did so he saw that Pryme was stretched out next to him, her eyes closed. Her golden body was drying, but a few drops of water exaggerated her bronzed skin, laying like diamonds set in bronze.

"I was programmed that way for the nursery and the primary class," Ega answered, "it is amazing the questions that children can come up with, so the drones have to have all of the answers."

"Was Pryme a good student?" Stef asked. Stretched out on the warm sand, under a warm sun, listening to the warm tones of the drone, he felt sleepy.

"She asked more questions than any other child." Ega's voice was beginning to recede, "It was for that reason that I was attached to her permanently." Stef fell asleep!

He awoke soon after with a start. Pryme and the drone were exactly where he had last seen them, and Benza was stretched out on the other side of Pryme. Ega had thrown his clothes over him, so he stood and put them on. The clothes were dry, and so was he.

"I covered you to stop you burning," Ega said, "It can be quite painful, I believe!"

Sleepily from his other side, Pryme stirred, "I could do with a cool drink."

Ega opened a box she had brought and produced two glasses and a bowl, presumably the last for Benza. From a flask, she poured clear water into the vessels. She held one up for Stef.

"Thank you Ega!" he accepted the glass and marvelled at the coolness of the liquid. Then he remembered the incident and eyed the glass closely. Here in this simple liquid was both life and death! It was something he must remember; things not as obvious as they first appear, then he remembered Control's words, 'Try not to see the obvious, and extend your thinking beyond today.'

Pryme sat up, "We will have something to eat, and then we can explore some more!" she decided. She donned her garment while Ega served out the food. Benza ate from Pryme's fingers.

CHAPTER TWENTY

"I don't think we have ever come this way before!" Pryme said. They had walked for some hours, but not actually marched; Pryme kept darting off the well-defined track to point out something to Stef, and even he soon picked up on the game. He marvelled at a butterfly's wing pattern and the tiny centres of flowers that held their own secrets. He remarked on the variety of birds, from the small to the largest. They were so unused to humans that Stef could approach one close enough to see their dark eyes.

Then Benza barked and poked his head into the grass; he had found something. At first, Stef could not make out what had attracted the dog, and then he made out the furry outline of a tiny creature with its prehensile tail wrapped around a stem of grass. Pryme pulled Benza back, and they both bent down to examine this tiny creature. It stared back with enormous dark eyes, and at the end of its quivering nose, its whiskers fluttered. Above the face were two huge ears. Then in a flash, the tail released its hold on the stem and the creature vanished.

"It was possibly a mouse, but what kind I cannot tell," Ega informed them.

"Are there many kinds?" Stef asked.

"Hundreds, possibly thousands!" Ega answered, "There are also similar creatures that are not of the same family as mice."

"Incredibly small!" Stef said, "Did you notice his tiny hands and fingers?"

At this point they stopped and had something more to drink, this time a pale pink fluid that was incredibly

124

sweet, so much so that Stef had to cough. Benza had slurped some water out of the bowl and run ahead.

Stef looked at the sky. The sun was past the zenith but it would be several hours before darkness, but they had also walked a long way.

"Should we turn back now!" he asked.

"Why? It is a beautiful day, and we are having such fun!" Pryme danced after the dog. Reluctantly, Stef followed her, and Ega brought up the rear. They were travelling towards a headland that jutted out into the lake. It had a copse of tall, straight trees leading almost to the strand of beach, and Stef guessed that they would see more of the lake once they were there, maybe the rest of the lake.

He heard Benza barking, perhaps he had found another mouse, but there was something different about the noise. Stef looked up and saw that Benza had almost reached the trees and had met another dog; what he was listening to was the barking of two dogs. It did not sound any worse than Benza by himself, and they appeared to be dancing and running round each other, just as Benza ran around Pryme when they were playing. Then Pryme appeared, running towards the two dogs.

He turned towards Ega, "I think that Pryme may be in danger, after all, we know nothing of this other dog!"

"I cannot detect any aggression in the dogs, in fact, they appear to be overjoyed!" the drone answered, "The problem is when dogs hunt in packs, and this is a solitary animal."

Stef quickened his pace to bring him up to the noisy dogs, only to find Pryme already there and playing with both dogs. He slowed when he saw that there was no danger.

"Look at these two!" Pryme was obviously delighted to find another dog. They had been sniffing at each other, then at Pryme, and now turned their attention on to Stef and Ega. The other dog was almost identical to Benza in size and colour, but the patterns of colour were different. The new dog spent a longer time with Ega, taking an extra sniff, probably because the drone was so different.

"What are you going to do now?" Stef asked, "Two dogs might be a problem!"

The new dog suddenly darted off with Benza following. They raced along the sand and disappeared around the headland, so Pryme started after them, and Stef and Ega had no alternative but to follow. When they arrived at the point, they found Pryme standing and staring down the lake. Indeed, as Stef had surmised, much more of the lake could be seen, but what he had not expected was a small building with smoke rising from a stack on the roof, and a man sitting outside and playing with both dogs!

The building was not like those of the City; it stood alone a little way back from the water's edge. The man was sitting in an old chair, by the side of which was a table and a bottle and glass. Obviously, he had been relaxing on the porch, when his dog brought his new friends.

On seeing Pryme and Stef approaching, he stood and waited for them. He had a half-smile on his face, and if anything his skin was even darker than Pryme's!

"Hello there! Are you from that monstrosity?" he called out.

"If you mean the City, yes!" Stef answered. Now that he was closer, he could make out that the building was made of wood, and he remembered that in the films he had seen these and that they were called shacks. When he looked up the word it said that it was a temporary building, but this looked as though it had been standing a long time, long enough to warrant repairs. Now that they were closer, Stef could see that this was a very old man, his long wild hair merged into his white beard. Eyes were the bluest that Stef had ever seen, and they were set amid many wrinkles in a mahogany face.

The man nodded, "I guess it is the only place you could be from!" He stopped as Ega came in view to stand next to Pryme. "You are a drone! What on earth is a drone doing with humans?"

"What on earth are you doing living in the Outside?" Stef returned the question.

"Never expected to have guests, so there is only one chair if the lady would like to be seated." He did not answer the question but politely offered the single chair to Pryme.

Pryme shook her head, "No thanks! My name is Pryme, this is Stef, and the drone is Ega, my maid."

"Maid?" The man looked at Ega, "This is the first time that I heard a drone called a maid, but then I suppose things have changed in the City, and probably not for the best! My name is –"he paused, "Arn. It is a very old name, older than the City."

"It's very nice to meet you Arn, but I can see a fallen tree over there and we can all sit on it while we talk." Pryme pointed to a log by the side of the shack.

"That's not fallen!" Arn said forcibly, "That's felled, and all by me!" In an unspoken agreement to sitting on the log, he picked up his bottle and glass, "Sorry, only one glass too."

"We have some cups, so it is no problem!" Ega said, and Arn swung back and stared at her.

"First time I ever heard one talk as well!" He shook his head in disbelief and led the way to the log.

CHAPTER TWENTY ONE

Once they were seated, Stef started asking questions.
"How long have you been on the Outside?"

Arn scratched the whiskers on his chin, "Can't give you it exactly, but it was a long time ago. Came out here with my brother Kam!"

"So there are two of you?" Pryme said.

"Dunno! Kam went off on some fool idea, and I have never seen him since. You are the first people I have seen since then!" Arn looked down at the two dogs and ruffled their heads, "If it weren't for Basa here, I think that I would have gone mad!"

"Why do you choose to live out here?" Stef asked.

"Why not?" Arn chuckled, "There is nothing to do in the City, the drones do all of the work, and there is as much company in there as there is out here!"

Stef pointed to the shack, "So you built this, and you have to provide everything to survive?"

Arn nodded, "Kam was around at the beginning, and we built the home together, but I did all of the repairs. Basa catches things and brings them home, but there is a lot of things in the Outside to eat, if you know where to look."

"We know!" Pryme said, "We have been making things from materials out here, and we cook from what we find!"

"All three of you live out here?" Arn asked with surprise.

"No!" Stef shook his head, "These two live in the City, but their apartment is open to the Outside. I have been asked to find out why!"

"Who asked you?" Arn asked sharply.

"The Control Central!" Stef answered.

"Oh, him!" Arn spat, "He is the one who ruined the City, taking away all of the joy and fun!"

"Oh, I could not agree more!" Pryme burst out, "It is so grim and lifeless!"

"Well, he has no power out here!" Arn sounded slightly angry, "There is nothing here that he can control, but I was alarmed to see a drone here. You're not planning to ruin this as well?"

"Oh no!" Ega stepped forward, "Stef just has a job to do, and it is about us, and I would not allow anything to happen out here!"

"You would not allow!" Stef raised his eyebrows, "You are just a drone! How can you alter the outcome of something that Control wants?"

"Drones are the ones who control the City; we do all of the work!" Ega said, "Nothing can be achieved without the drones!"

For a moment, Stef thought of the two drones working in the garden. They were certainly not in the City, but he said nothing, just stored that thought until later.

"Well they are welcome to it!" Arn retorted.

"Do you know of anyone else who lives on the outside?" Pryme asked.

"That was what Kam thought, and why he went rushing off!" Arn waved his arm towards the far end of the lake, "Damn fool! If there are others, then he is living there, or more than likely he was attacked by something!"

"Then you do not think there is anyone else out here?" Pryme said, and Arn replied with a shake of his head.

"We will not disturb you," Stef promised, "but we may come and visit from time to time if that is alright with you."

"Oh I don't mind!" Arn answered, and then with a glint in his eye, "Have you ever tasted smoked fish?"

"What are smoked fish?" Stef asked.

"Creatures that live in the lake," Arn said, "If you can catch them, they're awful slippery, they can be quite tasty. Here, I'll give you some, and you can see for yourself." He walked into the shack and came out with a handful of what looked like brown leaves.

Ega stepped forward and took them, "Thank you Arn! I shall prepare them for the evening meal."

Stef stared at the dried fish, "These live in the lake?"

"Yes, there must be thousands in there," Arn took one from Ega, "You must slit them open and take out the innards, cut the head and tails off, and you can cook them as they are, or smoke them for a day or two."

"Smoke them?" Stef was still puzzled.

"Get some wood shavings and burn them slowly, just smouldering with lots of smoke. You do that inside a small space like that," he pointed to a tall box-like structure at the side of the shack, "hang the fish high up in the smoke, and they take on an added flavour. You'll see!"

Stef stared at the lake. Far beneath the shiny surface was a world he did not imagine could exist. He nearly drowned in the lake, so how did these fish survive? He would ask Control later.

Ega looked up at the sky, "We must leave now before it is dark!"

Bidding Arn a warm goodbye, they called Benza, who was reluctant to leave his new friend, and they hurried back along the shore towards the City.

"What do you make of Arn?" Stef asked as they walked along the darkening path.

"In what way?" Pryme asked, "He and his brother did not accept life in the City, and I can understand why." She looked intently at Stef, "I think that you can understand that as well!"

"In a way I do, but to live just with a dog as sole company, it must be hard!" Stef said.

"People did that in the past," Ega informed them, "They went exploring, and finding new places and people, and a lot of it was done on foot."

"Just as we have done today!" Pryme observed.

"Yes, but civilization was never too far away!" Ega said, "And there is home. Do you want me to prepare the fish?"

"We can try it, can't we Stef?" Pryme looked at Stef for confirmation, and with a slight hesitation, he nodded.

"We can at least taste some of the fish," he said.

Pryme and Ega disappeared inside the apartment, and Stef sat on the bench. Benza came and sat next to him, so he stroked the ears and made a fuss of the dog. A few days ago he would never have thought that he would be able to do that, but a few days ago he did not know that there were any dogs left on the planet, and now he knew of two!

His thoughts went over the day. Finding Arn was a surprise, and Stef wondered about that. What were the chances of stumbling across the only person living in the Outside? Pretty slim chances, and that worried him! He was sent to sort out the question of Pryme, and that developed into questions about the apartment, drones, even about Controller and the City, and now in the same vicinity, there was another strange occurrence of someone living totally in the Outside.

He would have to cut this visit short, reluctantly, and turn the investigation inwards. He was sure that the answer lay within the City. Somewhere he had not been before or even suspected existed.

CHAPTER TWENTY TWO

Stef was quite sure that the answer to all of the questions lay within the City, why the City was built, and why there were drones. For two days he wandered around his apartment and even ventured through the grey echoing corridors lost in thought.

Pryme was a distraction, part of the puzzle true, but diverting his attention away from the real problem. He was very sure that the City was started long before the idea of The City as it was today was formed. It had been created in a chaotic time when people suffered and died in a myriad of senseless ways. Then something happened that started a transformation that created the drones, or perhaps that was accidental or coincidental. Almost certainly the drones were responsible for the shape of the City now and probably aided by Control. He was also certain that there were many Cities, he lived in one and Pryme lived in another; the length of the journey time between them indicated that.

The one vital question concerned the reason why the City was built, what was the danger that everyone hinted at, and was that danger still current? Eventually, he asked Jol where he could find anything about diseases, or natural disasters in prehistory.

"Golly! I have no idea!" Jol covered his mouth with his hand to hide his amazement. "I am not sure that anyone has researched those subjects, possibly because they are so unattractive!"

"It could be the key to the whole question, the anomaly that I was sent to answer in the first place!" Stef said firmly.

"I would have no idea of where to begin," Jol shook his head, "nor can I think of anyone to ask. I can go down to the archives and see if there is something to pick up, but I suspect that it will take some time."

"I am sure that it will!" Stef nodded slightly, "If I am right, it has been well buried for several millennia!"

Stef left the historian in deep thought. Jol was disturbed by Stef's reasoning; if there was something deadly many millennia ago, surely it could not still be a threat, or there would be nothing in the Outside. That may not have been the reason, or the only reason that the City was built. He sat for a long time looking at pictures of happy, suntanned people that drove around in ancient vehicles on makeshift roads, trying to bridge the gap between then and now.

Eventually, he stood and made his way to the huge sorting place, where drones retrieved documents from the past. He stood looking down the immense hall, and besides the drones there were a few historians, so he sought out one that he vaguely knew.

"Hello Pok!" He surprised the bald-headed man. Not many people spoke to each other in the archives under the City.

Pok stood up and turned, a sheaf of papers in his hands, "Oh, hello! It is Jol I think, yes it is, I remember. How are you?" He looked defensive, clutching the papers to his chest.

"I am quite well thank you. And you?" Jol gave the other historian what he hoped was a friendly smile.

Pok waved at the piles of documents behind him, "Tolerably well, but this is an unending task. Can I help you?"

Jol was sure that Pok could help; he was one of the oldest people down here, possibly three times older, and most of it spent in the sorting.

"I am looking for information about pre-City, up until the drones appeared." Jol looked down the ranks of drones, and he remembered a phrase, 'Through the mists of time.' He thought that was appropriate to the view; all of the documents were historical in some way or other, and here they stretched off into the misty depths. A thought came to him.

"Where do all of these documents come from?"

Pok pointed into the dim distance, "They emerge down there and arrive here on a conveyor. I do not know anything about pre-City, I think that you should talk to Kaa, he is over there somewhere." He finished by pointing to where a group of drones were gathered round a human.

Jol walked down to the group of drones, but before interrupting them, he stood and considered the far invisible distance. He wondered what was beyond the far wall, if there was a wall! In all his years no one had ever asked where the material came from, and it never diminished in quantity, if anything it had increased!

He looked at the drones and the strange looking human in their centre. Kaa was one of the tiniest people that he had ever seen, barely coming to Jol's waist-level, but despite his reduced stature, he was commanding the drones with authority.

Jol asked his question. "Do you have anything on pre-City or the earliest parts of the City?"

Kaa did not appear to hear him, directing a drone to move some files. Then he turned and looked up into Jol's face.

"What exactly are you looking for?"

"I am trying to discover why the city was built, and how and why there are drones," Jol looked hopefully at the diminutive researcher.

Kaa shook his head, "I know of nothing in that area! I can give you a tremendous amount before the City, well before, and some shortly after the City was formed and drones appeared. There is nothing about why!"

"It is just something that I wondered about," Jol said, "It is as though it was a dark age, and it needs some illumination." He wondered if that sounded plausible, and Kaa appeared to accept the explanation.

"I have thought about that period as well," Kaa took something from a drone and held it up against the light, "You do realise that was a period when there were great changes, and that many records were lost, or simply not recorded. There was something about the drones, how they were designed," he frowned for a few moments, "I wonder who it was that took that material."

One of the drones uttered a scratchy comment that Jol could not make out, but Kaa looked hard at the drone, "Are you sure?" he said and the drone uttered a short word.

Kaa turned to Jol, "This is most peculiar! This drone says that it was a fellow I have not seen for a long time called Kam. I remember now, he made a hell of a commotion, got very excited. If you can find him, he may have more to tell you."

"Where can I find this Kam?" Jol asked, and the drone gave another scratchy speech.

"This drone believes that Kam had a brother and that both stopped functioning a long time ago, that usually means that they died," Kaa explained, "You will have to ask Control as to their whereabouts. Good luck!" Abruptly he turned back to his task, and Jol walked slowly away.

He turned back and stared at the dwarf for a moment, but he had disappeared behind a screen of busy drones. When there was something unknown, most historians would show enormous interest, but Kaa just switched off his curiosity, and if it was not for that drone there would have been nothing revealed. It was such an obvious question that Jol wondered why he had not thought of researching it, but even when Stef brought up the subject, he found excuses not to get involved too much, if at all.

As he walked back to his apartment, he wondered what Stef would make of this. It would appear that this character Kam was a dead end, in more ways than one!

CHAPTER TWENTY THREE

Stef had a whole new set of questions on his mind, and now that he had sent Jol after the answers to the original questions, he could concentrate on the new puzzles. The main one was Ega; why was she so different to other drones? He did not accept that this was because she was an attendant in Pryme's nursery, for there must be thousands of similar drones looking after the infants, but none like Ega.

He took the long journey to Section AO356-12-54992, but when he stepped out of the bubble he paused, looking carefully at his surroundings and ignored the invitation of the open door. All of the surfaces were seamless, even the floor, except the moving pathways. Bending down he tried to find where the static floor stopped and the moving part began, but the division was blurred, as though the floor had decided that this part should move and not the other, but floors do not make decisions.

A movement caught his eye, and when he looked a drone was standing at the end of the platform as though waiting for him. For a brief moment he thought that it could be Ega, but she would not have waited without speaking.

"Are you waiting for me?" he asked.

Instead of the pleasant warm tones that emerged from Ega, this drone produced a scratchy, metallic rasp, and at first he could hardly make out the words. Obviously, this drone's speaking mechanism was hardly ever used. Eventually, the words made sense.

"I am waiting for you to move on your way, as you are blocking a delivery."

Stef had a feeling of embarrassment. He was occupying the space needed for the drones to accept something, and he was hindering their work.

Automatically he apologised, and then cursed himself for apologising to a drone. However, he stepped on to the moving pavement. As he moved, he looked at the structures around him. None of them looked exactly functional, and if he were designing this city, he would have filled many of the empty spaces; some were just a few metres high, while others soared to the roof. That produced a frown; was this a sign of Control's dysfunction? If it was, then it had begun long ago!

Then another thought came to him; where did that drone come from? There was no other opening, but there could have been one that melted into the structure, as many doors did in the City. The drone had just appeared; it did not glide into view, there again, Stef was not looking directly in that direction.

With a start, he realized that he had reached his destination. His mind had been so occupied with thoughts that he did not remember very much of the journey on the moving pavement. The door slid open, but no one was there to greet him, but he heard laughter coming from the garden, so he stepped inside and followed the sound.

Pryme and Ega were playing with Benza; throwing a ball between them and the dog trying to catch it. Ega turned round as soon as Stef appeared, but neither Pryme nor the dog noticed his arrival for a few seconds.

"Good morning Stef!" Ega greeted him, "Do you wish for some refreshment?"

"Thank you! I would like to have some juice; any sort will do." Stef could not help but compare Ega to the drone he had encountered on his way here. His eyes followed her as she went to fetch the fruit juice. Did he imagine a slight girlish sway of the hips?

"It is good to see you again!" Pryme said, "Are you planning to stay for very long?"

"That depends on what else can happen!" Stef replied, "If it is alright with you, I would like to explore some more of the Outside."

"Wonderful!" Pryme threw the ball out into the garden and Benza ran after it. "He will play all day. Has anything new happened?"

Ega appeared with glasses and a container of juice, and as she laid the tray down, Stef addressed her.

"There are some things that I think that Ega can help me with." Ega turned towards him.

"I will answer your questions if I can." The drone answered.

"First of all, you are not like any of the other drones that I have encountered; you even sound more human. Why is that?" Stef sat down at the rough table as he asked, keeping his eyes on the drone.

"As I explained earlier, I was selected to be Pryme's companion when she was just a child. I have to sound like a human, so that is a large part of my programming." Ega surprisingly sat down facing Stef. Most drones would remain standing.

Stef nodded slowly before continuing, "I viewed this garden from my apartment, and I saw Pryme and yourself playing, but you were not a drone then, you appeared as a young woman. Can you explain that?" He thought briefly about the dream that preceded the image but withheld that.

"I cannot explain how your equipment performed in this way," Ega replied.

"But she is a young woman to me!" Pryme interrupted, "Perhaps my perception influenced the projection that you saw!"

"If that is the case, why should that be? What is happening that a false image appears?" Stef never took his eyes away from Ega, who sat like a human, her hands folded demurely on her lap. "There is virtually nothing about you that reminds me of a drone!"

"That I cannot help you with," Ega spread her hands in a very human gesture. Stef leaned forward and took one of the hands. It was warm and soft, and if he closed his eyes he could believe that it was the hand of a young woman.

"I thought that you would be more curious about my manufacturing skills!" Ega said, leaving her hand in Stef's grasp.

Stef looked at the face, and saw there, in the eyes, a warmth that he was sure he would not find in any other drone. The face was smooth, artificial, and yet there was something there that disturbed Stef that he could not explain.

"I found out that all drones are equipped with the basic programs to manufacture all manner of things, in fact you are all programmed to perform a large number of tasks, so I was not that curious." Stef reluctantly let the hand slip away.

"Surely a drone that looks after children should be more human than normal!" Pryme said.

"Oh I agree!" Stef nodded, "I wonder where this nursery is, and do any of the drones there appear as Ega does to us?"

"I could not tell you that," Ega said, "I have no abilities to understand human perceptions. You said that you wanted to explore more of the Outside, where in particular?"

Stef realized that Ega had changed the subject, but he let that go. "I am interested in the other direction, across the river. Is it possible to go that way?"

"Yes it is, but you have arrived late in the day for a long excursion," Pryme leapt to her feet, "Ega fetch some drink, there is no need for food as we will not be away that long. Tomorrow we can see how far we can go."

They took the trail that led towards the waterfall, and before long they heard its tremendous voice in the distance. Stef looked down at the cascading water and noticed that even the ground shook from the noise. A little beyond the waterfall, they came across where the river divided as though it was two rivers joining. Across the water were some stones leading to a shore that made for an easy and dry crossing. Further up they came across another set of stones over the second stream. Here the trees were dense, cutting out all sound of the waterfall and anything else.

He pointed down to their feet, "See here how the trail is regularly used, even through the trees. There must be more creatures moving around than we are aware of." He turned back and looked at the stepping stones, "Those stones are very conveniently placed, but who placed them there?"

The trail led through the trees, and after a short while, Stef realised that there would be nothing to see in the time that they had. "I think that we should turn back." And so they re-crossed the streams and paused looking at the waterfall. Stef felt the mesmerising effect of the shimmering spray amplified by the shattering noise.

They arrived back at the apartment just as the sun was setting, the light bathing everything in a deep red. This was new to Stef and he kept stopping and looking at the changing light, so that they arrived at Pryme's apartment just as the sun disappeared.

Ega prepared a meal from the fish supplied by Arn, and at first Stef baulked at eating what was obviously a creature that had lived and breathed not so long ago, but after tasting a small part of the flesh, he ate all of it. Pryme had a similar reaction and only ate half of the fish.

While they relaxed and watched the sky, Stef continued with his questions and observations.

"I thought that I would have some pictures in the apartment of the outside world, to try and replicate your windows. Unfortunately, the Outside where I live is not as pleasant as it is here, which is why I ended up looking at your world and seeing Ega as a young woman. Then there is the length of time it takes to travel from my apartment to here; the bubble travels at an enormous speed, I am not sure how fast, but judging from the elapsed time, it is a very long distance." He took a sip from his cup of a tangy, smoky liquid, "I do not know how large this world is, but because of the different landscape and the distance, I do not think that the two apartments are on the same world!"

Pryme had her head on her hands, half sleeping and leaning on the table, but at hearing his statement, she sat up with her mouth open in surprise. "How can that be?" she looked up at the stars now appearing. "How can the tunnels connect two worlds?"

"I can see where Stef is going with this," Ega leaned forward, "The travel time is too great for a journey around this world, but what if it is not in a straight line; it could zig-zag back and forth, and it is possible that there are different parts of the world that are not as green and pleasant as this."

"That did occur to me also, but I have to consider all possibilities." Stef had kept his eyes firmly fixed on the drone, "There are also questions about where the drones came from and why, and why you are different to the others? You must agree that you do stand out from the others!"

"I am not complaining about her being different!" Pryme smiled at her companion.

"Thank you Mistress, it is nice to be appreciated!" Ega gave a little bow.

"I am sure that what Control sent me here to do was to reveal the reasons why the City was built, and why the drones are so important," Stef said, "I am positive that the two go together!"

"Why is it important?" Pryme asked.

For a moment Stef was stuck for an answer, then he said, "This is what I do, it helps to keep the City functioning!" Even as he said it, it sounded lame.

"I thought that this Control was perfect!" Pryme said, "But what you are saying is that things go wrong from time to time, and people like you are needed to repair things. From that I can take it that this apartment, Ega, and I are wrong, isn't that so?"

Stef stuttered, "No, you are not wrong, just not the same as others. I can find no statute that what you are doing is illegal!"

"I cannot see that being different is wrong either," Pryme said, "We are doing no harm to anyone else!"

Just as Stef was thinking of a reply, a dog bounded up to him. For a moment he thought that it was Benza, but then Benza appeared out of the darkened garden and he realized that it was Arn's dog, Basa. Stef peered into the night, but could not see anyone.

"He has followed our scent," Ega said, "That is how they hunt, but all he wants is another dog companion!"

"Shouldn't we take him back?" Stef asked.

"No! Very often Benza goes missing for a day or two, but he always comes back." Ega explained, "When they tire of playing they will probably go to Arn's place, and then back here."

It occurred then to Stef that Arn may be part of the puzzle. It is strange that he lives nearby, and had moved there many years ago, so how did he and his brother leave the City?

CHAPTER TWENTY FOUR

The party moved out in the morning, Stef, Pryme, Ega, and the two dogs. They followed the trail that led to the waterfall, crossed the two streams they had crossed on the previous day and continued through the forest. Stef found that the forest was creepy; he nervously looked around for a reason before realising that there were no sounds, even the two dogs bounding ahead initially made a crashing sound, but that stopped even though the dogs were in sight. For a brief moment, he imagined that he was the only person in the forest, or even in the world!

"What has happened to the sounds?" he asked his companions.

"It is the trees," Ega replied, "Their foliage and the wood itself are great insulators. Long before the City was even thought of, people would live in log houses for that reason."

"Like Arn's cabin!" Stef said in surprised understanding.

"Exactly like his cabin!" Ega confirmed, "Some people made wooden houses that were several floors high."

Stef looked up at the trees towering above their heads. He now began to respect the qualities of nature. As he stared upwards, he saw a creature with a bushy tail running along a branch.

"What is that?" he pointed at the creature.

"That is a squirrel, a small mammal that spends most of its time in the trees." Ega said.

"Are they dangerous?" Stef did not fancy a wild creature dropping on his head unawares.

"No! They eat mostly nuts, and they are nervous of humans, so they try to avoid us." Ega obviously had a huge range of information about the Outside. Then Stef realized that he was acting just like a child, asking all manner of simple questions, and Ega was drawing on her training and programming as a teacher.

As they walked deeper into the forest, Stef began to shiver; he had never shivered before in his life! Pryme had taken a coat from Ega and draped it over her body, and Ega was handing him something similar. He took it and wrapped it round his shoulders.

"The trees form a shield against the sun, and we are climbing higher, so we are cooling down." Ega explained.

"You said before that it becomes colder as we climb," Stef had stopped shivering and pulled the coat tighter around him, "Can you explain that?"

"The air becomes thinner as we climb, and it carries less heat because of that. Eventually it becomes cold enough to freeze water, and it also becomes difficult to breathe," the drone said. Stef then realized that he was panting from the effort of walking, and so was Pryme, but Ega showed no such difficulties.

Suddenly they emerged from the forest, and took in the view. Stef had the impression that they had stepped into space because the ground sloped steeply away from them, and far below the lake shimmered like a pool of silver.

Despite the sun's rays being uninterrupted, Stef drew the garment tighter around him; he was freezing cold!

"I didn't think that we had climbed very far," he muttered, "and I now do believe you that ice can form at high levels!"

"That is because we climbed slowly," Ega said, "If we had climbed directly upwards, you would have noticed the extra effort!"

Stef grunted an acknowledgement that he understood, and looked back to where he thought Pryme's apartment should be. He saw nothing that indicated that they stood on the City, there was just rolling hills leading down to the lake. He stared at the far side of the lake where there appeared a mirror image of the mountain that they stood on, and there was no indication that there was a City beneath the surface or just plain rock.

He voiced his thoughts, "Do you think that the City extends over the other side of the lake?"

"We have never crossed the lake, and as you can see, it is very large." Ega said, with a gesture towards the distance where the lake continued behind the opposite mountain. "We have no way of knowing."

Stef was beginning to warm up and he loosened the garment. Surprisingly, Pryme threw hers on to the ground and sat on it. She did not appear to suffer from the cooler air and persisted in wearing her usual insubstantial tunic, but for the first time she had covered her feet with some kind of shoes.

Ega set down the basket she was carrying, "Now would be a good time to drink something hot and eat something to replace the energy we have used." With that, she produced two steaming hot cups and some sandwiches with a strange sweet tasting filling. Stef ate without bothering to ask what it was, obviously something from the garden. The warmth of the drink made his cheeks tingle, and he could feel the warmth returning and flooding through his body.

He could see the garden, or what he thought was the garden, by the uniform rows of plants. When he was in the garden he had never noticed the regular patterns; he could see the two drones working away, and with a start he saw that further away there were more drones working outside. That was something to ask Elo or Control.

While he thought through his ideas, Stef had walked away from the others, and trying to see more from another vantage point. The dogs were having a mock battle, and he wanted a little less noise. Suddenly he received a blow in the back of his legs that sent him tumbling down the hillside, and when he stopped rolling, he stared up into the most peculiar creature; it has slightly larger than the dogs and covered with an off-white rough fur, but the feature that caught his attention was some bony sort of helmet.

The two dogs had raced over to this creature, barking as they came. The creature first faced them and then turned and ran off into the far woods. Ega called the two dogs back or they would have just kept on chasing. Pryme and Ega arrived at a slower pace.

"What was that?" Stef gaped after the white rump as it disappeared.

"That was a ram, a male sheep, and usually non-aggressive, unless there are others to protect," Ega informed him, "There should be some more over there where he went."

"What was it wearing on its head?" Stef scrambled to his feet and climbed back up the hill.

"It was not wearing anything," Ega actually giggled, "Those were horns, a hard bony growth that many male creatures have. Did it hurt you?"

Stef rubbed the back of his thighs, "Not really, but it tingles a bit. What is the use of such creatures?"

Ega pointed to Stef's costume, now covered with bits of grass and leaves, and the cloak she had provided. "That fur is keeping you warm. I made it from that creature's fur, and it is in your costume with other things. At one time everyone wore clothes made from that fur; it is called wool."

Stef examined the cloak seeing the fine strands that were woven together.

Ega moved towards where the ram had disappeared, "If you follow me, I will show you something interesting."

Stef followed but Pryme called the two dogs back. The ram had not run into the woods, but into a dip in the ground, and that is where they found it, surrounded by other similar creatures, some with horns and some without.

"This is called a flock, and he was just protecting them. They always keep together which is why it is easier to gather their wool." Ega pointed.

"How do you gather it?" Stef asked.

"I don't, other drones come out and do that!" Ega's answer stunned Stef.

"Other drones? I have just seen some more just beyond the garden, but I was told that there were no drones in the Outside!" Stef frowned and wondered why he was told a lie, or did Control not know of the drones activities.

"I said earlier that without their assistance the Outside would become a mess!" Ega turned to him and took his arm in a very human characteristic movement, "Some look after the plants and others look after the animals, some even keep the surface of the City in good repair!"

This was confirmation of what Stef had guessed at, there was work going on still by the drones, building and extending the City, but why was in not on the records? They walked back, arm in arm to where Pryme had fetched their cloaks and the basket.

"Do all of the animals keep in groups?" Stef asked.

"Quite a lot of them, for safety," Ega continued supplying information, "There are a few that are mostly solitary, and it is advisable to stay away from those."

"Wait until you see a deer!" Pryme held out a fresh drink to him, as he had spilt it when he was struck by the ram. "They are the most beautiful of animals, but they would do you more harm than the ram! Their horns are larger, sharper, and most delicate in shape."

Nervously, Stef looked towards where the sheep were grazing, out of sight now but uncomfortably near. He tried to dismiss any thoughts of the sheep and went back to inspecting the scenery. From here one had a different idea of the landscape. He compared the mountain that he stood on to the one opposite, and saw that there was a difference in the contours, the distant mountain had less rounded bumps; did that mean that there were no apartments underneath?

The lake curved round to disappear behind the headland where Arn lived, and beyond that more mountains and hills. On the surface, everything looked like a pastoral heaven, but Stef had a funny feeling that there was more hidden below the green foothills, and possibly the lake.

Ega called out if he was hungry, and so he made his way back to where everyone was sitting.

"You look very thoughtful!" Pryme said.

"Hmm!" Stef settled himself down, "I will tell you all that I have found out so far. Control sent me to sort out an anomaly, which initially turned out to be your apartment, then there came yourself, and then Ega, and finally Arn and his brother living in the wilderness. I tried to talk to an old friend of mine who works in City Control, and he denied that there was anything wrong with Control. However, there is something wrong, I viewed your garden and saw the three of you playing, but Ega was not a drone, you were a younger version of Pryme. Now, why would Control send me that picture?"

"Are you sure that was not a dream?" Ega asked.

"That is a weird thing!" Stef nodded, "Before that, I did have a dream where you were a young girl. I was not aware that control could read minds."

"Would it worry you if it could?" Pryme asked.

Stef nodded, "It would trouble me a lot because then I would have to ask what is real and unreal. I once ordered a meal as I do every day, but it was a magnificent layout for two that appeared, with silver and fine table cloth. When I asked Control about it, it denied it ever happened, even to suggesting that there was something the matter with me!"

Pryme had drawn up her knees and rested her head there, "I don't think there is anything wrong with you, but I understand your confusion."

Stef continued, "Then there is the question of the size of the City, judging by the length of time it takes me to get here, the City is larger than the planet, so I started asking about the early days and the reason it was built. I have asked a historian, you met him, Jol, to look into it, but we have found very little. The drones were introduced after the City was started, but have become vital to the functioning of the City. Every single thing in the City depends on drones. Before they appeared, people lived as you do, they drove around in open cars because the tunnels did not exist until after the drones appeared. What I have been told is that the City was built to protect us, but there is no mention as to what this danger was!"

"You have seen for yourself that there is very little danger in the Outside!" Pryme waved her hand at the scenery.

"Unless you are butted by a sheep!" Ega reminded them. "But that would not require a large city for protection, a fence would do!"

"Exactly!" Stef nodded and smiled, "Then we have Arn and his brother. How did they get out of the City? And judging by Arn, there has been no deleterious effects on his anatomy, and I suspect that he has been out here much longer than you. I have come to believe that Control sent me to understand what the City is for, its reason for existence. Why is the real puzzle?"

"Do you think that Jol can help?" Ega asked, "It has been an incredibly long time from what I have been told."

"I think that we can find enough to come to a conclusion," Stef nodded firmly, "We will also find out why you are an unusual drone, and Pryme an unusual person."

"I also think that you are unusual, too inquisitive," Ega said, "If you are satisfied with what you have seen, I think that it is time to go home or it will become dark before we arrive."

Stef was surprised by the suggestion that he was unusual as well. Had Control mixed together some unusual people, and for what reason?

With one last look at the flock of sheep, they turned towards the downward trail. Stef looked up at the frozen heights above them. Ega had said that it would be difficult to go there, even dangerous. For a fleeting moment he wondered if that was a danger, and then dismissed the thought, the danger existed before the city was built.

CHAPTER TWENTY FIVE

It had not become completely dark by the time they arrived at the apartment, and the air was still warm from the now disappearing sun, so they sat outside on the rough wooden table. Ega went in to fetch water for the dogs, and to prepare something for the humans.

"This is a strange task Control has set you!" Pryme said. The failing light bathed her face in shadow so that he could not make out her expression, but her eyes glowed like the embers of some long forgotten fire.

Stef gave a long sigh, "Yes! Control set me a task without defining the task properly, but I think that was also important towards solving the problem. I do not think that you and Ega, Arn and his dog are the problem, I am beginning to think that you are part of the solution!"

"Did I hear my name used in vain?" The voice came out of the darkness, and was followed by the sunburnt form of Arn. The dog Basa had sensed his approach, and unnoticed by them he had sped off to greet him and now danced happily by his side.

"I hope that I'm not intruding, but I thought that I should look for the dog, and I guessed he was with you." His friendly smile lit up his face. Stef thought that the sunburn made him blend in well with the night.

"Not at all Arn," Pryme said, "We were just discussing Stef's problem, and maybe we have nearly solved it."

"Could you tell me how you left the City?" Stef asked.

"That is easy," Arn settled down on a bench, "We think that for some reason a part of the building had not

156

been completed, at least it was open to the Outside. It was like that for a long time, long enough for my brother to explore several times before convincing me to join him. Since then the building has been completed."

"Have you any idea where your brother went to?" Stef asked, just as Ega came out with three plates of food.

"I heard your voice Arn, so I brought you some food." The drone said.

"Ah, it is always better when someone else prepares it!" Arn swung round and took the plate, "Thank you!"

"Your brother," Stef reminded him.

"He built a canoe, that is a small boat, and he rowed out into the lake, each day going further than the previous day, and then one day he never returned. I have no idea of what happened to him, perhaps the canoe sank, perhaps there was a creature out there that killed him, but I like to think that he found someone or something that was better than me." Arn took a mouthful of food.

"So you think that there are others living in the Outside?" Stef asked.

"Well, there is you, and there is me," Arn's eyes crinkled up in laughter, "So why should there not be others?"

The thought had never occurred to Stef, and it jolted his mind. He realized that he was accepting too much at face value without thinking deeper, exactly what Control had said. If there was one, then more could be an expected possibility.

While his mind raced over other things that he may have missed, Stef asked Arn, "Why did you leave the security of the City to live in the Outside?"

"It was all Kam's idea, and he did not try to explain fully," Arn looked thoughtfully at the contents of the cup that he had been given, "I always thought there was something he had not told me, and since I met you I think that he must have met someone or something. We had big arguments before I agreed to come here, but this was as far as I was prepared to go."

"So you think that he met someone out here?" Stef felt that this could lead somewhere.

"I am not sure, just a feeling that there was more to this than he let on," Arn gave a brief, sad sort of smile.

"Is it difficult to build a canoe?" Stef asked, but it was Ega who answered him.

"It depends what you call a canoe. There is a simple hollow tree trunk or a frame covered with some material, and both of those can have an outrigger, like another hull at the side to make it more stable."

"Would it take long to make one?" Stef began to form a plan.

"If I had the material, I could make one in a few hours," Arn said, and Ega confirmed that she could as well.

"Do you think it wise to follow in Kam's footsteps?" Pryme looked worried, "Look what happened to him!"

"I have to check in with Jol first," Stef said, "There is no rush, and we can be better prepared than Kam!"

CHAPTER TWENTY SIX

"My word!" Jol exclaimed, "You have been in the Outside again! Just look at how dark your skin is now!"

Stef looked at his arms and saw that it was becoming more like Pryme's, a golden glow almost appearing beneath the skin. Jol found a mirror and held it up, and a stranger stared back at him. If anything, his face was darker than his arms. He had made an appointment with Elo for a game on the courts, and he would quickly guess where Stef had been. He wondered if there was a way to disguise the tan.

"Have you found out anything?" he asked.

"Nothing positive, bits and pieces. Perhaps you can make sense of it." Jol scratched his head to show just how puzzled he was. "There is something I wish to show you before going any further."

Jol took him down to the collecting place where Kaa was still surrounded by drones, but Jol just stood back and pointed.

"This is where everything arrives and sorted out for us to find. As you can see, the drones do most of the work, but the question I have is where does all of this material come from?" He turned to Stef to see what the reaction was.

Stef looked at where Jol was pointing, "I see your point! How long has this operation been going on?"

Jol shrugged, "For as long as I remember, and I suppose since the City was built."

"That does not make sense!" Stef muttered, "There cannot be that amount of material to process!"

Jol nodded, "That was my thought, and Kaa there is not interested; he just works away without question."

"What else have you found out?" Stef logged that thought in his mind.

"Kaa told me of a legend that two brothers went to live in the Outside a long time ago, their names were Kam and…"

"Arn," Stef interrupted him, "I have met Arn and he still lives in the Outside. It is not a legend!"

Jol looked at him in open-mouthed wonder.

"I think the pieces are coming together!" Stef slapped the historian on the shoulder, "I think that Control sent me to investigate the Outside and the City, but I still do not know the reason!"

Jol had still not closed his mouth, and seemed to have some problem in speaking.

Stef continued, "I am relieved that it is not Pryme and Ega, although they are part of the question. Now what is the real question?" He slapped Jol's shoulder again, "Close your mouth, I have a lot to deal with now, and we are on the proper path for the first time!"

CHAPTER TWENTY SEVEN

Stef requested a cream to cover his suntan, which he applied to areas that would be visible. It was not perfect, but it was less noticeable, and he ordered a sports overall and a mirror. He looked at his reflection; he had put on some extra muscle, probably from all of the walking in the Outside, and with some misgivings he travelled to the sports hall.

"About time!" Elo said as he caught sight of his old friend, "The others are already playing, so we can sit this one out. Jek and Yop said that they may come later."

Stef sighed with relief that Elo had not noticed anything unusual, and he would also have some time to talk to Elo while they watched the game. Surprisingly, it was Elo who started the conversation.

"What was all of that stuff about Control going to pieces?" He said as they took some seats looking down into the arena. There were four players who held rackets, large energy fields attached to their hands, which they used to divert an energy 'ball' into the opponents goal area. The floor of the arena was not flat, it formed the bottom half of a sphere, and the players could run over all of its surface.

Stef thought for a moment, caught off guard by Elo's timing. "I have been trying to find out about the beginnings of the City. It was something that Control sent me to do and it developed from there. There are a few odd things happening, but I think Control knows about them, maybe he has even engineered them!"

Elo glanced sideways at his old school-friend, "You caught me half asleep, so it didn't fully register at the time, but a few days later I appeared to take the wrong journey, and I could not find a reason for that. It was then that your words came back to me, and I have been sniffing around."

Stef made a silent O with his mouth, and then spoke, "You put me off that morning, but you are right and there are several things that you should be aware of, but first I have a question, do you know how long the tunnels stretch?"

"All over the City, obviously!"

"How large is the City then?" Stef countered.

Elo blew out his cheeks, "Now you are asking! It is big, huge, that I know! Why are you asking?"

"I have had to travel by bubble to a destination that is far away, but at the speed they can travel, I could circle the planet in minutes, but it took many hours to get to that destination. I think that it is on a different planet!" Stef was not surprised at the reaction his words caused. Elo looked absolutely stunned and said nothing.

"There are people living in the Outside, and I have spent several days there myself!" Stef's words did the impossible, Elo moved his mouth and nothing came out. "If you don't believe me, you can come and see for yourself!"

At last Elo's brain caught up with his mouth, "Outside, people! You think that this is a design by Control, but why?"

"Ah, that is the problem," Stef rubbed his hair, "I believe he sent me off on an investigation that would eventually reveal the answer to that question. It has to do with why the City was built, and why the drones were created. Do you know that I have met an amazing drone that can do almost anything, and knows a huge amount of information, and she talks and acts like us?"

"She?" Elo's eyebrows rose, "Drones do not have a gender!"

"Meet this one and it will change your mind!" Stef gave a snort, "There is also an old man that lives by a lake in the Outside. He has lived there for years by eating what grows there."

"Forget the game!" Elo stood up, "We will make some excuse and go back to your place. Is that make-up you are wearing?"

Stef glanced at his hands. He had been rubbing them together as he talked and the tan was showing through. "Yes it is! If you spend any amount of time in the Outside you will turn brown."

Elo was impatient; he pushed Stef to make him walk faster, "You can tell me more as we travel. This is the most fun I have had for years, ever!"

Gone was the staid official that followed the teachings of Control, the laws and regulations, now Elo was once more the schoolboy, the companion in fooling and larking around mischievously. Stef tried to fill in the story, but Elo had so many questions that the tale became disjointed.

They arrived at Stef's apartment without the full story being told. Before they entered, Stef placed a hand on his friend's chest. "This will seem strange to you, but I have permanent furniture; I just said that I do not want it removed every time. Pryme's apartment was created by her drone Ega, and cannot be removed."

Elo entered and eyed the furniture, the paintings on the walls, and finally stood before the 'window'. "If I

163

didn't know you better, I would call a psychdrone! You think that everyone lived like this in the past?"

"I do not think that but I know they did!" Stef ordered another chair for Elo, "We can take a short trip to see the historian Jol, and then down to the archives to see the historians at work. If you feel you can face it, we can then take a long trip to Pryme's place and walk in the garden. I warn you that it can be traumatic!"

"First, show me the research results," Elo settled himself in the armchair, "Then we can decide on the next step."

It took many hours of showing, mainly due to Elo asking some very deep questions, and also his attempt to understand the basic way of living in the past. Like Stef, he was captivated by the photograph of the couple standing in the open by the automobile.

"They look happy!" Elo said unexpectedly.

The idea of what the figures in the photograph felt had not occurred to Stef before. He looked again, "I suppose that they do, certainly not uncomfortable or frightened!"

Elo turned to him, "Frightened! Why would they be frightened?"

"There are several references that the City was built to protect us, and that it was not fully successful until the drones appeared." Stef explained yet again.

"Then I think that we should inspect the Outside together!" Elo said, "Perhaps together we can solve this mystery. Is the only way out through Pryme's apartment?"

"As far as I know, but the old man and his brother must have used another way." Stef replied, "He never said where it was, except that he once tried to find it and it had disappeared."

"Well, we can find it later," Elo said, "Now we can see this amazing garden!"

Stef gestured towards the 'window', "That is it, that is Pryme's garden! For some reason it selected and fixed itself on that spot."

Elo looked at the garden, "I wonder if that is something that Control is arranging? Incidentally, I never said, but there are some weird things happening that is worrying my colleagues, but I now think that it is Control deliberately doing these and that there is nothing wrong with him!"

"Now it is my turn to ask you," Stef said, "Him! We always give Control a gender, but as far as I know it is a machine."

"Oh Control is far more than a mere machine!" Elo smiled slightly, "Control is a thought, an idea that has developed over a considerable amount of time, even longer than the age of the City. Why it happened and who created it we do not know, we do not know where it is located, and it has the unique ability to self-repair."

"Then what do you do?" Stef asked, "I was under the impression that you were working with the machine, actually touching it!"

"It gives a series of calculations, which we feed into the City machine." Elo smiles, "We check every calculation which has always proved to be flawless, that is why I said that Control is never wrong!"

"Just a moment!" Stef pointed a finger, "Control gives you calculations that you feed into the City! I was always under the impression that Control and the City were the same, but now you tell me that Control Central is something outside of the City, they are different entities!"

"To most people that would mean nothing," Elo said, "But in the context of your task, now our task, it makes a world of difference!"

Stef nodded, "It does, and it is too early to leave to see Pryme, so we can invade our historians! I'll tell him to meet us." He left a short message with Jol and they made their way by bubble, there was enough room for them to sit side by side, but neither of them had travelled with anyone before, at least not since school days.

Jol was waiting for them at the entrance to the archives, and they entered, once Elo had been introduced.

"It is probably not very interesting to you," Jol apologised, "but to people like me it is endlessly fascinating!"

Elo waved a hand to dismiss the apology, "I understand, but there may be other things here that would interest me, they certainly attract Stef!" He looked down the line of drones and historians.

"This material is sorted and taken to the archives over there," Jol pointed to the tidy racks and bowed heads of the historians, "We all have different interests, but not many of us appear to be interested in the time before the City."

"Nor was I until Stef started asking questions!" Elo shook his head, "What we have is something that I expect is mind blowing, and I am not sure that I want to know what it is!"

They walked down the line and observed Kaa and his drones working away, but then Elo's eyes looked further down to where the endless stream of material appeared. Without saying a word he turned and walked to where the historians studied in less haste and noise.

"I would never have guessed that there was so much industry in the City!" he said, "Nor that there were so many interested in history, but ignoring the most important features."

"That was one of the things that struck me," Stef said, "Everyone was very busy avoiding the most vital questions!"

Jol looked from one to the other, his eyes wide in astonishment, "Do you really think that this matter is that important?"

"If I am not mistaken, what we find will change all of our lives!" Elo said so softly that his words could be just heard. "I understand that you have some maps of the old City, shall we look at them before we take a long journey to the Outside?"

Jol led them to his apartment. Elo stood on the threshold and observed the clutter in the room, the documents pinned to the wall and the overflowing secretary and desk. Jol cleared the desk and produced the oldest map of the City. Stef pointed out the features, and Jol produced photographs of smiling people in their daily pursuits.

"All of these look happy!" Elo pointed out, "There is not one sad face, no terror of fear, and so what was so terrible?"

"As far as I have found out, it is so obvious that it is invisible!" Stef said, "I am glad that you have come here Elo, we need several pairs of eyes to see the obvious!"

"Well, I think that it is time to visit this Outside and see what there is!" Elo said.

"If you don't mind, I have a fear of open spaces, so you will have to do without my eyes!" Jol said with a nervous stutter.

CHAPTER TWENTY EIGHT

Leaving Jol looking anxious, possibly afraid of what they would find, in the City or in the Outside, Elo and Stef took to the bubble again.

"Now settle down," Stef reminded Elo, "It is the longest journey that I have ever undertaken! You can watch a play, two or three if you want!"

"I have brought a book!" Elo produced a foil from his pocket, and when he opened it, it hardened into a flat surface, on which words appeared. Stef had no use for books, and he was surprised that Elo had.

They settled down, Elo reading with occasional snorts and brief laughter, and Stef trying to ignore him and listen to a broadcast. The walls of the tunnel sped past without notice, and without marking the progress of time. Elo and Stef both dozed when they tired of what they were doing, until a slowing of the bubble woke them up.

"You were not exaggerating when you said it was a long journey!" Elo said as he stiffly stepped out of the bubble. After stretching their legs and stamping the circulation back, they took the moving pavement and arrived at their destination, the door opened and Pryme was there to greet them.

"Welcome! You are Stef's friend Elo, please come in and make yourself comfortable!" She waved them in. She still wore the diaphanous garment that revealed far too much of her body. Elo looked and turned to Stef with a mischievous smile that reminded Stef of their schooldays.

"I see what you mean by turning brown!" He then turned to Pryme, "Thank you for your hospitality. Stef here needs to clean himself of that awful cream!" He wiped a finger over Stef's forehead to reveal brown skin.

"Why would you do that?" Pryme looked puzzled.

"A brown skin would stand out in the City, and I have no intention of attracting attention!" Stef said defensively.

As they moved into the room, Elo's attention was drawn first to the windows, and then to the figure standing just inside, Ega.

"You are the drone that I have been told has made all of this, is that so?" Elo asked.

"Welcome! That is true," Ega's mellow tones raised Elo's eyebrows, "I took the materials from out there," she gestured towards the windows, "and I made everything that you see here. My name is Ega!"

"It is unusual for a drone to be so human, and even more unusual to have a name!" Elo said in a friendly manner.

"The name was given to me when I started in the nursery, and my voice was adjusted to be more pleasant to the children," Ega said, "especially Pryme!"

"Who is responsible for exposing this apartment to the Outside?" Elo said.

"It was like this when we arrived!" both Ega and Pryme said together.

"And you spend considerable time in the Outside?" Elo knew the answers but had to make certain.

Pryme answered, "Isn't it obvious from my skin and that of Stef's skin, once he has removed that cream?"

"I will fetch some cleaning things, or would you prefer a shower?" Ega asked.

"I think that I would take a shower, thanks," Stef answered and followed Ega into her side room.

Pryme turned her full attention on to Elo, "Stef told me that you work with the Control, is that exciting?"

Elo laughed, "Far from it! I would imagine that it is the most boring job in existence! Now show me this fantastic garden."

Pryme stepped through the window, and Elo followed after making sure this was not an energy field that would be painful. Pryme stood by the crude wooden table, and gestured for Elo to take a seat. He looked at the trees, and then up in the sky where a falcon screamed. Despite being prepared for this, his mouth hung open. Pryme said nothing and just let him take in the vista.

He must have sat there for some time because his thoughts were interrupted by Stef and Ega returning. Stef's skin now had a golden sheen, and he had donned a costume made by Ega.

"You should walk down to the lake," Stef said, "It is not far, and you can get a better view of the Outside, but be warned, do not enter the water in any way!"

"Oh yes!" Pryme cried, "Ega, be a sweetheart and fetch some food, and we can go and see Arn. I think Elo would be most interested in meeting him! Where is Benza?"

"I think that he is off playing with Basa," Ega said.

"Who is Benza and Basa?" Elo asked.

"Dogs!" Stef answered him, "They can look ferocious, but they are very playful."

"They are animals?" Elo was starting to show signs of overload. It was starting to stress him out as it had effected Stef earlier, and Stef took one arm, and Pryme took the other. Perhaps human contact would help.

They came to the water's edge, and Pryme carried on walking until she was up to her knees, then she turned and smiled, "This feels wonderful!"

Elo did not try to see how wonderful it was. He turned and looked at the birds floating on the water, and watched as they took flight. "I have seen this on old films, but it looks more incredible in real life!" He flapped his arms in imitation of the birds.

They kept walking towards the headland, and halfway there the two dogs came racing towards them. Elo looked dubious, despite everyone saying that they were just greeting them. To show that there was no danger, Stef started vigorously rubbing the dog's ears.

"Where did you get them?" Elo asked.

"They live out here with all of the other creatures!" Pryme said as she started playing with the dogs, "He came to us as a baby, a pup, and now he is part of our family."

The dogs raced ahead, and they followed slowly. Stef pointed out the mountain behind them, "That covers the City; it is the City or at least a part of it!"

Elo no longer looked shocked; he even fondled one of the dogs ears when it came racing back. Maybe it was because Stef was there, someone he knew for a long time that he was making a faster adjustment than Stef had.

"That is where Arn lives!" Pryme said as they rounded the headland and the shack came into view. Arn was standing outside, obviously warned of their approach by the dogs.

CHAPTER TWENTY NINE

Elo had never seen someone so old and wrinkled and dressed in a mixture of hand-made clothes and skins. Despite that, the handshake was strong and firm, and the blue eyes that studied him were bright and clear.

"Welcome, welcome!" Arn said, "I am just doing a spot of fishing." He pointed towards the shore where four poles stuck out of the sand.

"Fishing, what is that?" Elo and the others walked over to the poles.

Stef explained, "There are creatures in the water called fish, and they are edible. This is obviously how Arn catches them."

"Here, you can see what I caught so far," Arn showed them three fish that he had laid out on the bank. Elo bent down to examine them, but one was not dead and made a leap into the air that startled everyone. Elo sat down heavily in surprise.

Stef walked over to the poles and observed that they were not just poles, and neither were they simple. A fine line ran from the tip into the water, and the tip was made from a thin reed.

"That is to tell me when there is a fish on the line," Arn came up behind him, "Look at that one, see how it is vibrating and twitching. Well, that tells me there is a fish there." He took hold of the pole with both hands and gave it a sharp pull. "Yup! Here it comes!" Stef noticed then that the line was wound round a cylinder, which Arn was winding as fast as he could. Within moments another fish lay flapping on the bank.

"Why would the fish bite the line?" Stef asked.

"Here I will show you," Arn fiddled in the fish's mouth and produced a small hook. "I will now put something tasty on the hook, and throw it back in the water. The fish thinks that it is dinner when it is the fish that will become dinner!"

Elo had been standing close and observing everything that Arn did and said, but he made no comment.

"Well, we do not need your fish at the moment," Pryme said gaily, "Ega has brought enough food for all of us!"

"Ah yes! The clever drone who is almost human!" Arn said with a smile, and he did not sound unkindly.

"Thank you Arn!" Ega said, "We did eat the fish that you gave us, and I am told that it was delicious!"

Elo spoke out to Ega, "Do you ever wish that you could taste food, and have emotions like us?"

"As a matter of fact, I do have something like your emotions, or I could not look after humans, especially children!" Ega's remark caused a long silence, and Elo did not comment, although there was an expression of surprise on his face.

"Surely you cannot taste!" Stef said.

"I said something like!" Ega said, "I can identify certain tastes so that I know not to feed children something that would harm them."

"There seems to be a lot more than we thought concerning drones!" Elo said, "Are all drones capable of these things?"

"All drones are exactly the same," Ega said, "But not all of the capabilities are switched on with most drones."

Elo gave her a hard stare, "Who switches them on?"

"As far as I know, it is Control!" Ega replied.

Elo continued staring at the drone for a few seconds, and then transferred the same gaze to Pryme and then Stef. Obviously some very serious thoughts were passing through his mind, and probably similar to Stef's thoughts about what Control was doing.

"You came here with your brother?" Elo turned at last to Arn.

"Yes! Kam had some strange ideas, and eventually, I came out here with him." Arn replied.

"He was a historian," Stef said, "We found that out at least!"

Arn nodded, "He found something there that got him so excited, but he never told me what it was."

"How did you leave the City?" Elo probed further.

Arn scratched his head, "It was a long time ago, but I remember that we walked down a passage and at the end it was open to the Outside. By that time Kam had started to build this cabin, but it has been repaired many times since."

"Your brother left here?" Elo asked.

Arn nodded, his expression was neither sad nor happy, "Yup! Made a canoe and sailed down that way several times and then one day he never came back! Dunno what happened to him!"

"There are no brothers in the City!" Elo was glaring at him, "As you well know, children of the same parents do not stay together, so you would not know if he was your brother of not!"

"That is true Elo!" Ega interrupted, "but a brother can mean a very close friend, brothers in spirit!"

"I always said that we were brothers, "Arn nodded in agreement, "We were almost alike in our ways, except Kam was more adventurous."

Stef looked meaningly at Elo, "There is something that he found in the archives, something so important that he dragged you out here, and I would dearly love to find out what that was!"

"Where did Kam live in the City?" Elo asked.

"I cannot remember!" Arn shook his head, "There has been no need for such things out here."

"We can check with Control later!" Stef said, "Are you hoping that he left some clues, and what would happen to an unoccupied apartment?"

"I have never come across a reason to ask that question, all of the apartments are occupied!" Elo frowned; for a moment there he thought that he would have a quick answer to his questions, and Stef's!

"Oops! We got another fish!" Arn broke the spell and grabbed one of the poles.

Stef was glad of the distraction as everyone turned to watch Arn deal with the fish. He needed some time to deal with all of the information and decide what to do next. Although he thought that Kam's apartment no longer existed, at least as Kam's, he would have to check it out. Now he realized why Jol had been steered in his direction, part of the answer lay in the archives. He would have to have a long discussion with the historian to find out if there was any record of Kam's work, as he realized that he could not rely on Control as a reliable source.

As they all walked back to Pryme's apartment, including Arn, Stef was uncommunicative, almost brooding as he ran things through his head, on the other hand Elo was chatting away to Pryme and Arn. It was Ega who walked with Stef, the drone seemed to sense that he was troubled by events. In a surprising human gesture, she linked her arm in his. Stef just gave her a weak smile.

CHAPTER THIRTY

The meal was a mixture of Ega's prepared meal and Arn's fish, and some peculiar things he called nuts and beans. Stef took what was handed to him but just nibbled at the food; he wanted to get back and talk to Jol, but he did not want to show how urgent it was.

Eventually Elo said that he had some work to do early in the following day and bid everyone a good night. Stef gave them all a wave and followed his old school-friend to the bubble. In the bubble, Elo was talking but Stef feigned sleep, and very quickly he really did fall asleep. He dreamed of Ega mostly, again as a young woman, and she was with him in the archives, leading him by the hand towards something, something that was infuriatingly out of focus; as his hand reached out to take it, it moved further away. Then the bubble came to a stop!

Bidding Elo farewell, he first called Jol but found that he was in the archives. Still, with the dream of Ega in his mind, he took the short bubble trip and made his way down to the archives. At first, he could not see Jol, but then he made him out, talking to someone and waving his arms in excitement. As Stef drew near, he saw that the other person was Ree who was trying to calm down Jol.

On seeing Stef, Jol waved a paper at him, "This is the answer; this will tell you all that you want to know!"

Ree waved Stef forward urgently, "Take him away please, he is causing too much noise!"

Stef took the historian's arm and led him away from the group of disconcerted readers that had started to object. Jol was bubbling with excitement, "This is amazing! Never would I have thought it!"

"Keep your voice down, and show me outside," Stef said. When the door closed behind them, he turned to Jol, "What is all the excitement about?"

Jol held up a bunch of papers, "This tells us that the City was not originally designed to be enclosed and that it was changed when the drones appeared. It was them that enabled this to be done!"

"That's fine, but does it say why they appeared and why the City is enclosed?" Stef asked, "I already know that the City and drones go together, but I have no idea why!"

Jol's face dropped, and the excitement faded from his eyes, "No, it does not, but I thought that you would be pleased!"

"I am!" Stef stated, fearful of hurting his friend's feelings, "All I had was a suspicion, but now you have found the proof, and that is most important!"

Jol brightened up, "What did you find?"

"That the drones are most important," Stef said, "Without them, this City would not exist!"

"So our findings agree!" Jol looked happy and surprised.

"But we still need to know why!" Stef rubbed his face with both hands, "I need to really think this through. The questions are now, what is Control? What is the City? And where do the drones exactly fit in?"

"You are no longer interested in the original questions?" Jol asked.

"In part!" Stef took a deep breath, "They are minor in comparison, and those answers will fall into place as part of the whole! I am going to my apartment my friend; I need to rest and think this through."

He accompanied Jol part of the way to the historian's apartment, but Jol stopped suddenly and pointed up at the soaring concrete above their heads.

"See those odd levels? I am no designer, but I always thought that they represent a waste of space; if we were to maximise the space effectively, there would be fewer levels, and I am right! I have found out that those flat tops were once gardens, full of flowers, and people walked in those for leisure. We did once enjoy nature!"

Stef looked up, and in his imagination he could see the people walking, laughing through beds of bright scented flowers, and not only there but also in the streets that are now empty, echoing chambers. A shudder ran through him; there were ghosts that now moved silently in a dead landscape, and he could envisage in his mind's eye trees and flowers filling the void; a line he had read somewhere entered his mind, 'The Hanging Gardens', although he had no idea of what they referred to.

Stef walked into his apartment and stared at the furniture as though he had never seen them before, and the question came, why did he order these? He rubbed his temples and slumped in the armchair, and soon he slept. Once more it was Ega as a young woman, leading him towards a door that receded as they walked towards it.

There must have been more to the dream, for he awoke with a start bathed in sweat. What had he dreamed that could startle him awake and make him sweat? He ordered a shower, and stood for longer than usual, letting the water sooth his mind, then dressed in a new overall he sat in the chair again.

"Control! Why are you teasing me?" He called out in the empty room, "You send me on a task in which you already know the answers!"

Control's voice filled the room, "I knew that you would reach this point eventually and that you would raise questions about everything around you, including me, but your task is not quite complete!"

"If I run through what I think, not what I can prove, would you correct me?" Stef asked.

"Up to a point!" Control said, "To complete the next stages will take longer than your life many times over, but you must realise the sufficient of the truth to be able to take certain actions correctly."

"Okay, I think that the City was started for another reason," Stef began, "it was not originally intended that the City should be enclosed, we lived in the Outside, and then for a reason I have yet to discover, the City was enclosed when the drones appeared, without them the task would have been impossible!"

"You are correct!" Control confirmed, "But I will not fill in the parts you have yet to discover!"

"I am not asking for that," Stef said, "I would like to know where the drones came from, and I suspect that their origins were as different as the reasons to create the City. While we were enclosed, the Outside became the abundant green world we see today, probably more than it has ever been before, and now for some reason you want us to live in the Outside again. One reason I have been given for the enclosure is that there was a threat that threatened everyone, and now that threat no longer exists!"

"The threat was real, and it still exists, but for your survival, you will now have to venture into the outer world, into the unknown!" Control's words had a very ominous tone.

Stef paused for a moment. This was not as he had expected! "If the threat still exists, then why should we seek the unknown?"

"That will become apparent to you in due course!" After this, Control would not say another word.

He tried to fathom out the meaning of Control's statement, but his thoughts were interrupted by a call from Jol.

"I have just found out something that has me totally confused! Can you come to my apartment?"

"What is it?" Stef asked, annoyed to be interrupted.

"I would rather that you came here!" Jol sounded as though he was in distress, so Stef said that he would.

It was obvious that Jol was agitated; his hair was a mess, and his lips trembled. He placed a hand on his forehead as though it ached. "I saw this a few days ago, but at first it made no sense to me, and then I found a little more information, and then it hit me!"

Jol removed his hand and looked into Stef's eyes, "We have only been collecting information for a few generations, and that historians are a recent innovation. We have only scratched the surface in that time!"

"I have been talking to Control, and he says that we must now change and start to live in the Outside!" Stef said, realising that Jol would not be able to face that prospect, "I do not think that we should abandon the City, just that more should live in the Outside."

Panic had filled Jol's eyes; his whole face was quivering, "I think that I could not do that!"

Stef placed a hand on his shoulder, "I do not think you will have to, just most of us, in any case you have still a lot of work to do in the archives, but it starts to make sense; your task is something fairly new, and Control said that we must now change, which can mean that this change has been in preparation for a reasonably short time! I have to find out was this danger could be!"

Jol looked relieved, "I really can't do what you do, but I will happily work anywhere within the City."

"I will have to collect a few things, and then go and have a really long talk with Pryme and Ega, especially Ega; I think that she could solve the whole problem!"

Jol unexpectedly change the subject, "Have you ever been to a nursery?"

Stef was taken aback, "No! Well, I must have been at some time, but not since I was a child!"

"I think that you should visit one before seeing anyone else, and I will come with you!" The panic had left the historian's face, and now he looked determined.

CHAPTER THIRTY ONE

Stef did not know where the nurseries would be, but Jol had prepared for this and led the way. "I thought of this some time ago, but never got round to it, but now is the right time!"

They did not need to take a bubble, just the moving pavements. Stef wondered if the historian was nervous about the tunnels as well, but shrugged off the thought. It did take some time to get there, but perhaps the nurseries were not connected to the bubble system, after all, it never occurred to him to visit a nursery.

As the door slid aside, a drone was waiting for them. It was indistinguishable from any other drone, but Stef had become used to Ega's pleasant tone and assumed that was what all nursery drones sounded like, so it was a shock when this drone spoke.

"It is unusual for humans to want to come to the nursery, it has not happened for a very long time!" The voice was still metallic and scratchy, but slightly better than the other drones he had spoken to.

Jol stepped forward, "We would be pleased to see what you do and ask a few questions."

The drone waved them forward, "I cannot see why you would want to do that. It is well known that humans cannot bring up children!"

Both Jol and Stef stopped dead in their tracks, surprised at the statement. "How are children brought up, and why are humans unsuitable?" Jol asked.

"You are too emotional!" the drone said, "You also cannot control your prejudices, and pass all of these and other deplorable things on to the children!"

Stef began to feel his temper rising; who was this drone to criticise them? The drone continued in its flat, scratchy voice preventing him from making a retort.

"Your history is full of war and bloodshed, and why is that? Because you are greedy, selfish, egotistical, fools! You are prejudiced against anything that is different, whether it is colour, language, or intelligence!"

Stef exploded, "Look here! I do not have to listen to this nonsense! We have not done any of these things, they was long ago!"

"Indeed they were, and that is because we have prevented those ideas from reoccurring, but I ask you now, what are your feelings towards drones?"

Jol nodded and placed a hand on Stef's sleeve to stop him answering, "We are guilty of thinking that you are less than us, although I think that may be changing. We have been speaking to one drone who calls herself Ega, and she is having an effect on our preconceptions."

"We know of Ega!" The drone said, "You give that drone a gender, how quaint! Perhaps it is influencing you thinking, but that is two from the legions of humans!"

"We did not give her a gender or a name, I believe that was done by her charge, Pryme," Stef had calmed down, "I begin to see what you are referring to, we cannot control what we think, and we speak what we think, and the child hearing this is influenced. So how do you bring up a child?"

"With difficulty!" the drone answered, "Human children have a propensity to fight over the most stupid of things, so we have to watch carefully to prevent that happening, and by the time they reach an age when they can reason, they are prepared to live a peaceful existence. Have you ever hit anyone with your fist?"

Stef blinked, "No, of course not!"

"That is due to our methods of child care," the drone turned away, "I think that now you can appreciate what you are going to see, and I will warn you not to utter a sound, or do anything that the child can experience and carry forward into their maturity." The drone walked forward and led them into a play area where some children of about the age of seven or eight were reading.

As soon as they entered, the children looked at them with a strange expression. The drone explained, "They have never seen an adult human, not one that they remember, so you look a little grotesque to them. In a moment or so one or two will come up and ask you questions, such as what is your name and what are you. You may give your names, but you should answer that you are simply large children to the second question, anything else I will answer for you."

In a few minutes as predicted a boy came up to Stef and craned upwards on his toes to look into his face, "Who are you?" he asked.

Following the instructions, Stef replied, "I am Stef, and this is my friend Jol!"

"Why are you so tall?"

"We are big children." Stef dutifully replied.

"But you are taller than him!" the boy pointed a finger at Jol.

The drone took over, "Do you remember that we said that everyone is different? Well, in a few years you will also be of different heights, just as you have different colored hair and eyes."

"So you are older than us?" the boy looked from one to the other, "I am Jek, and I will be different too!"

"Yes Jek," the drone said, "Go back to your reading, while I talk to these large children."

Jol was amused, "It is a long time since I was called a child!"

"We try to keep everything as simple as possible at this stage," the drone said as they walked away, "In a very short while that group will begin to question everything, it is called puberty!"

Stef smiled, "I think that I recollect what that was like!"

"Yes, it is a difficult adjustment for humans, and it is when they become particularly aggressive, especially the males, although the females have a unique method of aggression." The drone stopped walking as they reached the passage, "If you have further questions, perhaps now would be a good time to ask them."

"When do you select them for their later education?" Jol asked.

"We already have by this age!" the drone said, "Everyone has innate abilities, things that they do because their brains are wired in a particular way, and these become apparent quite early on, but we do not force them."

"So you already know what their studies will be, and later their occupations?" Stef said.

"Of course!" the drone pointed to Jol, "He has different interests to you, but also different to other historians. That makes for a richer world."

Stef nodded, "And since drones are all the same, the children are brought up in a stable atmosphere, except I know of one drone that is not the same!"

"You are referring to Ega of course!" the drone said, "We are all capable of doing what she does, but that was because Pryme was an exceptional child, and it was decided that Ega would remain with her charge and that they develop together. You have noticed how human she is?"

"I understand now, she is as she is to be a capable companion to Pryme!" Stef said, nodding as the pieces fell together,

"And to keep her out of trouble!" The drone said, "You have noticed that Pryme is unusually free in her manner. We do not know why that is, so Ega is her companion and her guard!"

"Who decided that?" Stef asked.

"Why, it was Control of course! She is kept under observation all of the time!"

Stef frowned, "Do you mean that she is a prisoner?"

"I am surprised that you know the word," the drone gave a scratchy laugh, "She is not locked up in a cell, but she is guarded day and night."

"One last question," Stef said, "How did you know that Jol was a historian?"

"Jol spent his early years here, in these rooms, and we follow all of the children's progress."

"What do you not know?" Stef asked.

188

"Someone once said that there is no limit to the things one should know, and we know only a fraction of what there is to know!" The drone bid them good day and turned away.

CHAPTER THIRTY TWO

"What did you make of that?" Stef asked Jol as they travelled back on the moving pavements.

"I think that the drones are responsible for many things that we are not aware of," answered Jol, "If you think of it, the drones do everything; they mend things, build things, educate us, and keep everything running, but we are hardly aware of their existence!"

"It is all done out of sight, so we do not realize their contribution," Stef wondered if that was a part of the problem he was sent to correct.

"What are you going to do now?" the historian asked.

"I am even more convinced that I should have a long talk with Ega; if anyone can explain what is happening, it must be her!" Stef said with a determined edge to his voice.

"I am almost wishing that I could come with you." Jol's statement surprised Stef, but he continued, "But I know that I would fall to pieces!"

"Never mind my friend, I think that you are doing marvelous in the archives!" Stef slapped Jol, on the shoulder.

"What are you going to talk to her about?" Jol asked, "I know what, but how are you going to get her to tell all, instead of changing the subject?"

"You have noticed that! Actually it is Pryme that keeps changing the subject," Stef said, "I think that I will have to talk to Ega alone, but she is always close to Pryme, and now we know why!"

"Come to my place," Jol said, "We can have something to eat and drink, and think what we should do."

Jol ordered the food and drink, but Stef just picked at the food, and said very little. He did not want this artificial food; although it was very nourishing technically, it was not very exciting, and he said nothing as his thoughts were miles away. Jol realized and said little as well, what was on his mind was what would happen to him if and when the City opened up. Would they want or need historians?

Stef returned to his apartment and continued thinking hard. How could he get Ega to open up? Eventually he heaved himself to his feet and took the long journey by bubble to Pryme's apartment.

To his surprise and annoyance, Arn had arrived and they we already into a long and humorous discussion, but he waited until the party ended and then he would talk to Ega, perhaps while Pryme slept.

Eventually Arn left, and Pryme turned her full attention towards Stef, "You are welcome to stay here, I am sure that Ega would make up a bed for you."

"I will stay a while longer," Stef replied, "But I will probably not be staying!"

"If you do not mind, I am going to sleep," Pryme yawned, "We have had a busy day!" She stood and walked to her bedroom. It occurred then to Stef that the apartment was much larger than usual; normally one room served all purposes, but since all of her furniture was created by Ega, they would all need separate rooms.

Ega stood before him, "What do you want to do?" It occurred to Stef that she had expected this and had prepared herself.

"Please sit down Ega," Stef patted the seat next to him, "I would like to talk to you. I have been to the nursery, and none of the drones there are anything like you; your speech is much more developed, and the things that you do are remarkable, and I think that there is a reason for that!"

"I told you the reason; it was to be a companion to Pryme!" The drone gave a very human shrug to her shoulders as she sat down.

"That is only partly true!" Stef pointed his finger, "I know that the City was originally designed to be open to the Outside, and that changed when drones appeared. I also suspect that you know a lot more than you are saying."

"Probably!" Ega said, and then appeared to change the subject, "Would you like to walk down to the lake?"

For an instant Stef grew angry at this attempt to avoid answering the questions, but then he had a second thought, perhaps this is Ega's way of giving an answer, "As long as we can continue talking."

"Of course we can," Ega gave a low whistle, "We can take Benza with us, and I'll take a light." The dog came bounding up to them and followed the drone inside while she fetched a lamp. When she appeared she had a strange contraption that actually used a flame, and seeing his expression, she explained.

"This is an oil lamp, and long before there was anything like electricity, people used these for illumination!"

Stef frowned, "It is not very bright!"

"It will be enough to see our way!" Ega replied, "Come Benza!"

As they cleared the grove of trees, Stef saw that the lake shone, and he looked up at the source of light, the moon, a diminutive shining globe. Even with the lamp and the moonlight, he still had to concentrate on where he was stepping. He wondered how anyone managed in ancient times.

"I was created a long time ago, long before Pryme was born," Ega began as they walked along, "It was also a long time after they started to alter the City. Do you know that whatever I make, it will always be different to the one before, but your replicating system will produce exactly the same thing time after time? That is the difference, and that is why I am slightly different to other drones; I came into being before the replicators!"

"Who made you?" Stef was stunned by that revelation, it would make the drone extremely old.

"Humans, just like you!" Ega began to swing her arms back and forth, the oil lamp guttering and changing the shadows, and in the dim light, she no longer looked like a drone, she had morphed into a young woman! Stef shook his head; perhaps the dim light was causing his eyes problems, or perhaps it was because her movements were so human.

Ega continued talking, "At first no one realized that I was different, not until we introduced the nurseries, and started to educate the children properly. You really had no idea of how to bring up children! Our programming was opened up to release what had been put there much earlier, and then one or two of us excelled in the task."

"That was explained to me!" Stef shook his head, "The drone there said that we could not bring up our children properly, even suggesting that our system produced bad people!"

"That is true!" Ega took his arm, "It is difficult to explain about the way humans used to live, it was very precarious, hit and miss. One day things would be perfect, but the next day they could be plunged into all manner of terrifying experiences, victims of crime or warfare, and even more subtle experiences. Children are like damp clay and the impressions they receive are there for life!"

"I keep seeing you as a young woman, even the transmissions to my room of you playing with Pryme in the garden show you as human, have you any idea why?" Stef realized as he asked that this had been troubling him and blocking his thoughts.

"Not really!" Ega laughed, "To think of me as human!" She laughed a second time.

They had reached the lake shore, and the highlights on the water shone like burnished silver. The mountains that surrounded the lake were soft deep shadows of different shades, sculptures made of the night.

"This is magical!" Ega said, "Can you not feel the mystery and magic?"

"I thought that it would be silent, but I can hear noises!" Stef cocked his head to one side.

"That is the creatures of the night," Ega took his arm. Her artificial flesh felt warm against his. He had never felt a drone before. "There are just as many creatures at night as there is in daytime."

"What is that?" Stef pointed down the lake, "I can see a bright line moving this way."

"Ah, just wait!" Ega hugged his arm as they waited. Soon the white line drew opposite and Stef could make out ghostly white shapes. "Those are swans, giant birds that live on water but can fly many miles. They also swim very quietly! I will point them out to you in daylight."

"Why did you want to come down to the lake?" Stef asked.

"One reason is that the night sky is much clearer from here," Ega pointed upwards.

Stef looked up and his breath caught in his throat. Innumerable stars studded the darkness, and the huge band of stars that he had seen earlier, were far more prominent. As he looked he felt lost, as though he was floating in space.

"What you can see are two galaxies, the Milky Way, our galaxy, and the Andromeda Galaxy that are about to merge into one super-galaxy," said Ega, "and you can see that the stars have different colours, so they are not all white diamonds, some are sapphires and others rubies."

Stef was once more mesmerized just as he was the first time he looked deeply into the night sky, "How many are there?"

"Ah! Think of the biggest number that you know, and multiply it by a million!" Ega said, "There was something else. You went to the nursery, but did you go to maternity where the children are born?"

Stef came down to earth, "Maternity? I never thought of it!"

"You should have! You may have stumbled over something to help you realize how important creation is." Ega said. Stef knew that there was no more pregnancy as it were; as soon as the child is conceived it is removed and nursed until it is developed. There was no more nine-month term for the female to tolerate the pain and discomfort. He realized that Ega had a point, he, Jol, and Elo knew nothing!

While he pondered on that, he was distracted, "Look! There are some more swans coming!" He pointed down the lake.

"That is not a swan!" Ega said, "This is the main reason that I brought you here!"

CHAPTER THIRTY FOUR

"I do not know everything," Ega said, "but what I do know I will try to explain!"

"That is probably a thousand times more than I know at the moment!" Stef said dryly. For a moment he hesitated, trying to sort out which question was the most important, and then with a mental shrug realised that they all were.

"Where does Ook come from?" Stef asked as they continued to sit at the table that had appeared from nowhere. He wondered if it was permanent or a projection.

"That I do not know!" Ega said firmly, "What I do know is that from time to time he appears here, and I always know when, and before you ask, I do not know how I know!"

"From what was said now, I understand that the City was constructed to remove any inequalities and that everyone should be satisfied," Stef said.

"You have not got that quite right," Ega said, "It did remove any physical inequality, but people were far from satisfied, mentally or emotionally; that took a long time to solve!"

"What was the problem?"

"People need a reason, a purpose, and at first there was a lot of dissatisfaction, so we reinvented many of the tasks that people needed." Ega touched his arm, "If Control knows everything, so is there really a need for an investigator? I do not mean that unkindly, and I think that there is a reason now, today for you to enquire."

"What about the historians or Elia, what are their purposes?" Stef felt a strange drop in his mood as he listened to the drone's words, but he continued to ask questions.

"Would you be surprised that the historians are fairly new, just a couple of generations, and there has never been anyone before Elo and his team?"

Stef stared hard at the drone, "That can only mean that we have been brought together for the same purpose, but I still have no idea of what that is!"

"I cannot help you there either, as that was not included in my programming!" Ega apologised.

"What is Ook?" Stef asked, "He said that he was not human, but not a drone either! He is the oddest person I have come across!"

"I do not know!" Ega said, "I am sorry, but those are deep matters that I have not been informed about."

"I had the impression that he is close to Control: is he Control?" Stef rubbed his temples as he felt the pressure grow.

"I am sure that he is not Control," Ega said, "but I also think that Control has no command over him, nor he over Control!"

Stef tapped the wooden table, "Is this real, or something from the City?"

Ega bent down as though to smell or taste the surface, "It is real, but I am sure that it was not here before Ook arrived!" For the first time, the drone sounded unsure, puzzled.

"All that I can see is that the City was and is for the good of humankind," Stef said, "It stopped us from possibly destroying everything. I have seen some of those weapons and the result of using them, although I do not understand everything, I am quite sure that would have happened if Control and the City had not appeared!"

"What do you make of his remarks about the stars?" Ega asked.

Stef stopped and automatically looked up, "His last remark was that we are made of the same stuff as stars; how can that be?"

"Ah! There I can help!" Ega said firmly, "But it is difficult to explain, so we can do that a bit later. The other thing that he mentioned that is also difficult to comprehend was about people being dissatisfied, and that I can also explain for you, and right now!"

Stef looked at her, and in the dim starlight she appeared to have human features, "Okay, please explain!"

"Ever since humans appeared, there has always been something for them to do, or they would have starved, been killed, froze to death, and all sorts of dangers, and there were no cities, so they worked in groups, each individual being responsible for some aspect of the group's survival. At a later date when the risks were reduced, people had time to do other things, think about the stars, make paintings, invent furniture and vehicles, and in the end there were people who devoted all of their time to these, those things became more important to them, so that everyone had a task to do. The City and the drones took all of those things away, so they were reintroduced. People were going mad for nothing to do!"

"I would have thought that people would have enjoyed having nothing to do, especially something boring or difficult!" Stef frowned.

"At first everyone was relieved, but a few hung on to their old lives," Ega said, "then some started showing signs of mental stress, strange behaviour, even harming themselves. It was a sad time!"

"So you invented work for them!" Stef said and nodded in understanding, "Now that I know, I am not sure how I feel."

"Ah! You have a real purpose, even if you do not fully realise it at the moment!" Ega said.

"Can I share this newfound knowledge with Jol and Elo?" Stef asked, "I feel that I have to talk it through with someone other than you and Ook!"

"I will come with you!" Ega stood up, "There is still a lot to tell you!"

As Stef stood he involuntary looked up at the sky, and it occurred to him that the real story lay there, and why that thought occurred was another mystery.

CHAPTER THIRTY FIVE

"I don't believe it!" Elo almost bellowed.

"It does seem to be incredible!" Jol agreed.

"I second the motion!" Stef laughed, "But you should have been there, and then perhaps you would begin to believe!"

"You are the gentlemen that are going to find out!" Ega said.

They were all gathered physically in Stef's apartment. Some extra chairs had been ordered, and Ega had fetched some of her wonderful coffee; at least that produced comments of appreciation.

"Who is this Ook?" Elo asked, "Where does he come from?"

"I do not know," Ega admitted, "The last time that I saw him was when Pryme and I moved into that apartment."

"I wonder why he did not say everything." Jol said, pulling on his lower lip, "It would have saved a lot of time!"

"If he knows anything at all!" Elo grunted.

"I am sure that he is the key to my investigation!" Stef said.

"Do we have astronomers today?" Jol asked, "I have never encountered one!"

"What does astronomy have to do with the City?" Elo snorted.

"I was just wondering," Jol said, "Stef said that his last words were about stars, and I think that is important, perhaps he was suggesting a direction to investigate!"

All of the men turned and looked at Ega.

"I am not sure what he was referring to," she said, "I do know some astronomy, but his reference does not mean anything to me!"

"You have met this Ook before," Elo said, "What happened then?"

Ega shook her head, "Most of it was about the apartment and the area immediately outside. If it is of any use, I also believe that he knows what this is about! I also believe that he is far older than the City, so he holds the key!"

"Nothing can be older than the City!" Elo had his face screwed up in disbelief.

"Well, that is not exactly true!" Stef poked his friend in the chest, "The world must be older than the City, and that must include the Outside, and not forgetting the stars!"

"Hmm. That is an interesting point of view," Jol rubbed his chin, "We have always considered that the Outside meant just the surface of the planet, but what if it meant the stars as well!" He turned to Ega, "What was this about galaxies colliding?"

Elo turned white, "What is this? What galaxies?"

Ega nodded, "It is true! The cause of collisions between galaxies, and even individual suns and planets is gravity. They are attracted to each other and eventually merge to form larger galaxies, many planets usually disappear."

Elo's face was deathly, "And this is going on now, with us?"

"Oh yes!" Ega appeared to be very relaxed at the prospect, "It has been going on for thousands of years! They do not actually collide, although some suns will during the process; what actually happens is that they slide into one another and become one."

"Is this the danger that was being referred to?" Jol looked at each of them in turn.

"Perhaps!" Stef frowned as he tried to remember everything that had been said over the last few weeks.

"I do not see how we can stop the galaxies colliding!" Elo had started to regain his composure, but he was still struggling.

"I cannot see how the City could have protected us," Jol waved his hands, "One small City against the universe! Unless what I have read is wrong or incomplete!"

Stef turned to the historian, "But it is not a small City! Do you remember that I said that it took an enormous amount of time to travel to Pryme's apartment? So it must be huge!"

Jol shook his head, "I do not think that any City, however large can compete with the universe!"

"There is obviously a lot more to this than we can imagine," Stef looked at Ega and wondered if she was holding anything back, "Where do the drones fit into the picture?"

Ega stared back, "I am not capable of answering that, I was never told."

"I have found out that most of the employment that we do is something fairly new," Stef rubbed his temples as he felt the pressure grow, "In ancient times we did these jobs, but then it was all taken over by the drones, and it is only now that many of the occupations are taken by humans!"

"What sort of time scale are we talking?" Elo asked.

"I had not discovered when these things happened!" Stef had his eyes closed.

"I think that it may be just a few generations since historians were reintroduced," Jol could feel Stef's frustration, "So perhaps it all started then."

"Yes, I agree, but that means that Control has noticed that a change was needed a few centuries ago, and only now is it possible to take action," Stef opened his eyes, "If only I knew what that action must be!"

"I think that we need another conversation with Ook!" Elo said, "That is if he is as old as you say, then he must know a lot more than us!"

"I could look for anything in the archives on astronomy!" Jol suggested, "I wonder what else could be of assistance?"

"I would look for anything on rockets and space travel," Stef remembered, "and that may require a talk with that odd character, what was his name? Ah! Ree! He had all sorts of information on travelling to other worlds."

CHAPTER THIRTY SIX

Ega managed to convince Elo that he should go with Jol in the archives. It took some time for Jol and Elo to locate Ree, but they found him sorting out a pile of photographs.

"You should see this stuff!" He exclaimed as he waved a fistful at them.

"I am sure that it is very interesting," Elo said, "We are here to know what you have on space travel."

"Not here! It is all in my quarters," Ree looked perplexed, "It is all a bit of a mess you know, trying to understand what they were doing, and there are odd photographs that do not match anything else. Of course, you are welcome to see it all as soon as I collect this. Give me a few minutes."

It was only a few minutes, and he led them triumphantly to his quarters with his booty of photographs. It resembled Jol's apartment, untidy chaos, and extra chairs were summoned for his guests. It was obvious that he rarely had guests.

"Now, space travel," he muttered as he sorted through various piles of documents, "Ah, ha! Here it is!"

Elo took the first handful of documents. At first, he blinked at the page and then handed it back to Ree, "I cannot read that!"

Ree took the offending page with a frown, "Yes! Sorry! We need to put it through a translator. There were hundreds of languages in the past, but most of these are understandable."

Elo sifted through the documents, "I will take your word for it! Do you have any modern document that describes all of space travel?"

Ree looked shocked, "No, why should we?"

Elo waved the documents in the historian's face, "Because this is nonsense! Someone should gather the information and then place it in some order so that the rest of humanity can understand what happened!"

Jol coughed, "We knew this Elo, but everything is so fragmented we do not understand it ourselves!"

With a sigh, Elo sat down, "Then I think that we should now try and see how far we can get."

They spent many hours sorting the material; Jol tried to categories the photographs, while Elo sorted the documents with Ree translating and explaining. They cleared one of the walls and pinned the documents in some order, and then changed them as more data came to light. To these, they tried to add the photographs. Eventually, they had a story, but there was still a huge pile of data that they could find no place for.

"This is incredible!" Elo said as they viewed the wall, "There was a belief that we could reach the planets and stars before there was any mechanical transport!"

Jol nodded, "They had hopes, a sense of adventure in those days!"

"Dreams of better things!" Ree acknowledged.

Elo wagged his finger at the wall, "But they turned those dreams into realities, that is the amazing thing!"

Jol peered at the wall, "This appears to be the time that they stood on the moon. There were a lot of poems about the moon and stars, mostly love poems. I wonder if that was what drove them!"

Ree looked surprised, "I never thought of that! Were they romantically involved in exploring? Would that be powerful enough to drive people to leave their planet?"

Elo ignored their speculations and was looking at the other end of the wall, "I wonder why they stopped! According to all this," he waved at the rest of the wall, "it was a great success, so why are we not still travelling to the stars?"

Ree and Jol looked embarrassed and shook their heads. "Perhaps the answer lies in the stuff we have still to place in order!" Jol suggested.

With a slow nod, Elo agreed, "From what I have seen so far, the cessation of space travel occurred roughly at the same time as the City was built, so there must be some connection!"

"If Ree agrees, I can work with him and try to extend the story, and our knowledge," Jol said, "We may have to bring in others who have knowledge in other subjects if that seems a correct thing to do!"

"It seems to be something enormous to change our course from living on many worlds to living in one City!" Ree observed.

"Quite, quite!" Elo heaved himself to his feet.

"Is this the danger that Stef keeps coming across?" Jol wondered.

"More than likely there is a connection!" Elo thoughtfully stroked his chin.

Ree scrambled through a pile of papers, "I have some things here, but it is very confusing!" He held up a few sheets, "They talk about firing people from a giant gun at the moon, and this one is about a material that makes a sphere float to the moon, then we fire rockets, and this one is about some sort of elevator, but the final one mentions distorting space. None of it makes any sense!"

"Perhaps they are all different versions of space travel, a sort of development of machines," Jol took the sheaf of papers, "I have never heard of most of these and they appear to be fantastic, almost impossible!"

"Perhaps they are just different ideas and not reality at all!" Elo suggested.

Ree shook his head, "I know for a fact that rockets existed; there are photographs of the rockets and people on the moon and other planets!" He pointed to some pictures.

Elo studied them, and then gave a grunt, "I think that is proof enough, but what of these others; floating through space, and as for an elevator, I thought that it had to be suspended from a high point."

"There used to be a culture that was based on fantastic ideas, and they appeared in books and on films," Jol said softly, "Perhaps these are from that culture."

"Whatever they are, they do not provide an answer!" Elo growled.

"Stef is always asking for background knowledge," Jol remembered, "he thinks that it would provide a basis for understanding what happened."

Elo agreed, "He said the same to me, but what we have is a mess, there is one thing here, and another there, and none of it links up!"

"It would not have to link up!" Jol looked up from the papers, "There are different aspects of our civilisation. There are the tunnels, the drones, the city, the food program, and perhaps they link today, but in the past it was different. Remember the open vehicles, flying machines, ships and railways; it was probably chaotic with different systems competing for attention."

Elo looked surprised, "You could be right! We have to add space travel, wars, building on a tremendous scale, but I also saw smaller buildings in some of the literature. Perhaps there were other things that we have not come across yet."

Ree had been closely following what Elo said, and now he gasped, "I have some things that I was going to put back in the archives as they made no sense. There are mentions of people being invisible, and others that could travel through time. What if they were real? Can you imagine travelling through time?"

"No, I cannot!" Elo snorted, "Jol has just said that they romanticised a lot, and this has all of the hallmarks of being pure fiction!"

Jol was staring at the ceiling and obviously trying to remember something, "But what if they were not! I came across references that describe monsters of incredible size, and humans with wings. Perhaps some of these were real in the past!"

Elo shook his head, "I do not believe a word of it!"

Jol wagged a finger at him, "If we dismiss everything, we will dismiss the truth as well. I think that we accept all as possible for now, and then when we identify an obvious fiction, we can eliminate that and eventually we will produce a real picture of the past, or at least something close to it!"

"Hmm. I still think that this is a load of bunkum!" Elo's face reflected his words.

"Perhaps, but it will be up to Stef to put everything together, and he should have all of the information to do that!" Jol countered.

"You are forgetting this character Ook," Ree said, "He appears to know a lot more than anyone else, and that will sort out the truth from the fiction!"

"As long as he is also not part of the bunkum!" Elo gave a fierce grin.

CHAPTER THIRTY SEVEN

Ega and Stef wondered how to contact Ook. "I am not sure if he will visit us, as we cannot send a message!" They were walking down to the lake.

"I think that he will know that we wish to talk to him", Stef said with a quiet confidence.

Ega gave him an odd look, "I think that you are getting close to the answer to your quest! I also think that he will be there!"

"One thing does confuse me," Stef ran his hand through his hair, "Where does Arn fit into the picture?"

"Perhaps he does not fit in anywhere," She took his arm in hers as they stepped down the path to the lake, "He and his brother may just be accidental adventurers!"

Stef laughed, "Just a diversion to waste our time!"

"Not really a waste, no one that you meet is a total waste of time!" Ega said, "Every meeting is an exchange that enriches both parties. He certainly made you think!"

Stef laughed again, "I would never have thought of a meeting in quite the same way, but you are correct, he turned my views up-side-down!"

"And now Ook will turn everything in-side-out if I am not mistaken!" She pulled on his arm, "That is where we met him last time, so perhaps we should wait there."

"I think that you are right!" Stef pointed, "There is the table again, and that is steaming coffee! I can smell it!"

"But where is Ook?" Ega peered down the lake.

"Right here! I have been waiting for you!" The voice came out of the darkness, and Ook walked into the lit area of the lamp. He was dressed exactly as previously with the long black garment.

"How did you know that we wanted to talk to you?" Stef asked.

"That will become apparent to you as our conversations evolve," The ancient's eyes twinkled in the lamplight, "Lovely word that, 'evolve'."

"I have a small question..." Stef began, but Ook interrupted.

"No question is so small as to be insignificant!"

Stef continued, "... I thought that Control could not project anything in the Outside, but you have summoned a table, chairs, and some coffee. How is that possible?"

"The answer to your small question is that I am not Control!" Ook beamed at him, "All shall become clear, but we must progress in the correct order, or you will become confused!"

"I am confused already!" Stef said glumly.

"I know, and that is why I have appeared to smooth the path for you!" Ook patted the investigator's arm.

Ook settled himself into a chair and poured them all a coffee, and then he studied his fingers at arm's length, "One thing that I should make clear is that the drones appeared first, second was the tunnels, and finally the City. Without the first two, the City would have been impossible!"

"I have already decided that the drones came before the City, this City, but there was something planned much earlier!" Stef sat opposite Ook and took a sip of coffee.

The old man nodded, "But in a complex way, none would be possible without the other; they come as a package! I will have to go back a long time in human history to supply an understandable story. We, the humans evolved from the other animals, we are animals but very sophisticated ones, and a part of that evolution concerns the use of materials, such as food, building materials and fuels, but there is a finite quantity of any of these, and eventually there would be none, and the human race would perish!"

"Is that why food and other things appear on demand?" Stef asked.

"That is part of it, but let me continue," Ook paused and took a sip of coffee, smacking his lips with satisfaction, "When there is a shortage of any of these items, there will be wars, and the shortages appeared very rapidly. You would be surprised to learn that one of the shortages was living space! Every human needs a certain amount of space, not only for comfort, but to grow crops, mine materials, and for our own peace of mind, it was called 'living room', and when that became scarce, there were endless wars, but the main reasons were food and fuel. It was stupid, short-sighted, for every war consumed the very food, fuels, and living space that they were fighting for. Every war then led to the next!"

"Didn't they realise what they were doing?" Stef was incredulous.

"Some did, but they are things such as greed, not only for material gains but also for personal power gains, power over other people," Ook gave a weak smile, "There are many faults with the human race!"

"There was no Control in those times!" Ega spoke for the first time.

Stef paused for a moment, "Then who was in control?"

"Many kings, queens, emperors, presidents and chiefs and not many were as good as our Control!" Ook looked thoughtful, "If anything they were the greediest of all, but there were others who ran huge companies that were greater than the country they were in, and many of those were among the worst of all! They used up huge forests, drained liquid and solid fuels until there was very little left. Can you imagine a world without the beauty that you have seen here?"

Stef was taken aback, "Could no one stop them?"

"That led to some of those wars I spoke of!" Ook shook his head, "It is hard to believe that people ruled by fear using ignorance and stupidity, but they did! Very often a course of action was well under way before it was discovered, and then there were natural disasters!"

Stef never said a word, but his questioning expression spoke volumes.

"All of the time these human disasters were happening, Mother Nature supplied her own. There were volcanic explosions, earthquakes, tsunamis, diseases, and meteors. These things changed not only human history but world history as well, and there is very little that can be done to protect us from them! Finally, there is the sun and the stars."

Stef blinked and automatically looked up. The stars stared down, unblinking, unflinching, unmoving. What threat could they represent?

Ook read his mind, "They look beautiful, harmless don't they? But they are the biggest threat to all life, and the peculiar thing is that they also created life in the first place!"

Stef brought his gaze down and stared at the old man, "I heard you say that before. That we are made of the same stuff as stars."

Ook nodded, "It is true! Stars explode, and when they do they create new material, some of that is the stuff that makes trees, flowers and animals." He looked up, "From here they are stationary, immovable, and that is what we believed for a long time, but when out instrumentation improved it was noticed that there was an almost imperceptible movement, and when mathematicians worked out the details, they are moving at almost impossible speeds. The greatest and only reason is gravity. Everything has mass, weight, and that creates gravity, however small or large that item is. You have gravity because you have mass!"

Stef searched the sky and pointed, "Ega said that those are two galaxies colliding! Is that what you are trying to tell me?"

"In part it is, but there is a much larger picture." Ook took another sip of coffee.

Stef leant back in his chair and stared up at the stars. He could not believe that they were moving at any speed at all, let alone extremely high speed! Then Ook brought his thoughts down to earth with a crash.

"Of course you must realise that you are not looking at a real sky!"

Stef looked at Ook and then at the stars, and then back to the old man. Again he said nothing and just waited for the explanation.

"Just think for a moment," Ook started his explanation, "I have been talking about the human race running out of food, fuel and room to live a very long time ago, and by now all of it has been used up!"

Stef looked at the coffee mug, "Then what are we drinking? And what is all of that out there, the trees and flowers?"

"Ah! The coffee is actually energy, and that out there as you quaintly put it, is from another time!" The expression on Ook's face was one of amusement, but Stef did not even consider for one moment that the statement was not true, nor could he understand it.

The old man continued, "We ran out of everything long ago, including planets!"

Stef wondered if he had heard correctly, "How can you run out of planets?"

"To be precise, we ran out of suns!" Ook was holding the cup in both hands and staring at it intently, "All of the energy that we use originates from stars, but after every cycle, there is a bit less energy, and that has become critical."

There was a disturbance, and Pryme walked into the lamplight. Stef could hardly recognise her as she was wearing a standard coverall.

"Hello Ook!" she smiled at the old man, "How are you keeping?"

"Very well thank you!" Ook poured out another cup of coffee, "You are just in time to hear the complete story. This young man is already confused!"

"I am not surprised!" Pryme smiles at the investigator.

"I will start with myself," Ook poured some coffee for Pryme, "I was born a long time before Control was created, and I died soon after!" He smiled as Stef's gaped at the statement, "At that time I was as human as yourself, but many years afterwards the prototype of Control was created. The machine was originally created to quickly record details of an increasingly complex society, on the planet and in space. Humans had just started to explore the nearby planets. The machine was almost autonomous, as it would have taken humans too long to initiate any action, but how can a machine be believed? The answer to that was the creation of a woman, fabricated out of pure energy, and then myself, in a sense we were brother and sister. The machine chose me, someone who had died long ago, but was also one of the originators of the modern world."

"So you are a duplicate of the original Ook made out of pure energy?" Stef reached out and touched the old man's hand.

"Yes, and so are you if you understand the nature of matter and energy," Ook let Stef's hand touch and hold his, "In due time you will all learn about that! Without any recourse to a human agent, the machine reprogrammed itself and started on the journey that was to become Central Control, and that is pure energy that encompasses the entire universe, yesterday, today, and tomorrow!"

Stef fumbled with his cup, "Is that how he can manipulate time?"

"Only in part," Ook replied, "it was not until we began to use wormholes that Control came really into his own! I have a theory that Control's energy may exist outside of this universe, but I doubt that I will ever be able to prove it!"

The old man spoke all night until the horizon lit up and the stars faded, and the magical coffee pot never emptied or became cold.

CHAPTER THIRTY EIGHT

"Look at this!" Ree held up a document and Elo took it; Jol peered at it over his hands.

"It is a newspaper!" Jol exclaimed, "These were used before vidnews and were very popular. Oh dear!"

"Oh dear indeed!" Elo tapped the sheet with his finger, "This explains that there was going to be mass extinction, another since the beginning of time!"

"What is a mass extinction?" Ree asked.

"I have read a little on the subject," Jol rubbed his temple, "Every so often in the past there has been a natural disaster that almost wiped out all life. Fortunately, there has always been a few survivors. This one covers several planets at the same time, and that suggests something frighteningly powerful. Let me read some more." He removed the document from Elo's hand.

"Well, it could not have happened, as we are still here!" Elo smirked.

"It happened all right!" Jol shook the paper at them, "We just happened to avoid it by building the City! That is the reason the City was altered and became enclosed, but it does not specify what the disaster was, just a lot of stuff about radiation."

Jol turned the paper over, "There must be more of this; it finished mid-sentence!"

Ree shrugged his shoulders, "You know that we usually only find a small part of a document. Perhaps it is in this pile that I have yet to sort out."

Jol pounced on the pile, rapidly flicking through papers, photographs, newspapers, and even an occasional pamphlet. Ree looked on anxiously as his hoarded treasures were thrown to one side.

"Ah! Here is something about drones!" Jol peered at the print, "It says that there was an immense programmer to build hundreds of thousands to relieve humans from difficult and dangerous tasks. It would appear that humans were being killed in pursuing wealth and other things."

"Was that the radiation mentioned in the other paper?" Ree asked.

Jol shook his head, "It does not say, but it infers that we were working under ground and under the seas, even in space!" he paused, "In space! It appears that all of those children's stories were true after all!" he passed the paper to Elo and carried on searching.

He was stopped by the arrival of Stef, Pryme, Ega, and an incredibly old man.

"I would like you to meet Ook!" Stef introduced the old man, "He has explained our mystery, I think!"

"We know," Jol said, "There was dangerous radiation that threatened to extinguish life, and so the City was built to protect us, and the drones were created to undertake dangerous tasks!"

"That is almost correct!" Ook smiled at the little group, "Drones were around for a long time under different names, long before the City was considered in its initial form, and they were used in places that a human would not survive. Before them, Control was created by a very clever man, and before that was me!"

Ree had never met Ega or Ook, and he looked from one to the other with his mouth unlatched, "Th – that would make you impossibly old!"

"It would be if I were human!" The smile persisted.

"Wh – what are you?" Ree's stammer became worse!

"That is a complicated story," Ook cleared a chair and sat down, "Stef can explain that later!"

Stef held up his hands to stop the conversation, "We can come back to that later, but he has told us an incredible story, but I have seen the proof with my own eyes! Control, show the other galaxy!"

Against a wall, the night sky appeared with the giant arc of stars.

Stef pointed at the stars, "This is the danger that has threatened us in the past, and continues to threaten us today! That galaxy is colliding with ours, and when stars collide and enormous amount of energy is released. Most of the stars will not collide, but there will be enough to send radiation to kill all life on any planet within range, and that is nearly all. If the centres of the galaxies collide, it could mean the end of both galaxies, because that is where the majority of the energy exists!"

Elo studied the image, "That is going to kill everything?"

"That is what Ook has explained to us," Stef was very excited, "As far as we are concerned, it never happened, but I will let him repeat to you what was organised."

Elo swung round, "If it never happened, why all of the fuss?"

Ook coughed gently, "When it was first appreciated that the two galaxies were to collide, there was very little that we could do, we had not even flown into space at that time! We were using raw materials for energy, coal, chemicals, and oil, then nuclear energy appeared, but that was still wasteful and very dangerous. There were many theories about the nature of the universe, and over the years these were proved or disproved, but the big advance happened after nuclear fusion was created. This provided huge amounts of energy that was cleaner than nuclear fission, the stuff that explodes. By this time we had ventured into space and had colonies on other planets, even some circling other suns, and we began to think again about the other galaxy."

"I would have thought that you never forgot it!" Ree said.

"Some did remember, but we had other problems that needed answering, and much more urgent," Ook eased his legs, "At around the same time that the galaxies were colliding, the sun, our sun would die, and in the process it would destroy the inner planets and effect the remainder; it was a double problem, the sun and the galaxy, but we were in dire straits long before that! I could do with a drink; all of this talking is making me thirsty!"

A small table appeared next to him with a carafe of water and a glass. Ook poured out the drink and took a sip before continuing.

"There was a time that humans lived like the rest of the animals, and it is remarkable that we survived. One way was to build settlements and assist each other, that was called the Dawn of Civilization, and at first it was touch and go before it attained success. From that point onwards we began to dominate the planet; our numbers grew at an alarming rate, and when advanced technology appeared we plundered the resources of our planet. The distribution of those resources was uneven and many were in poverty; they died of hunger and disease, and of war. The increasing shortages for room to live, and food and energy caused many wars, each more vicious and terrifying than the previous war. We were able to harvest from the other planets, but this was extremely dangerous and expensive until someone discovered a way to make and control worm-holes; these are conduits of energy that enabled planets to be linked together in a huge network. In the beginning they were unstable, but when a way to control them was invented, it also enabled us to project to new planets. Travel times were shorter, and there was a peaceful period for civilization. The power to create this network was taken first from our sun, and then other suns as we expanded across the galaxy and beyond."

Ook stood up and walked back and forth with his head lowered, and his hands clenched behind his back. He stopped and looked at the image of the stars.

"One of the things we discovered when we used the worm-holes, what you call the tunnels, was that we were interfering with time. This is difficult to explain, but the result was that we could place things and people in different time zones, and we could create time loops where events were repeated in a never ending cycle. For eons the universe was repeating the same events and never moving forward, so the collision of the galaxies was postponed indefinitely. The City is a collection of places across the universe and linked by wormholes, the tunnels. As Stef observed, the time he took to travel across the City was greater than needed to travel across the City that he saw in the Outside. Only when he stood and looked at the City from a distance did he realize there was something strange!"

"So I was right! There are many Cities!" Stef said triumphantly.

"Yes! You just did not imagine that they were on different planets, although you did almost get there!" Ook nodded, "The time on the Outside is different to that inside the City; the Outside is in a time loop, while inside the City time advances as it normally does. But even this was not enough; we were draining the energy of many suns, and even if there was a time loop, each time it was repeated there was less energy available. Everything you are, what you do is based only on energy; even the Cities are made of energy!"

"Is that how we can summon food and furniture?" Jol had remained quiet, but he began to understand.

"That is correct!" Ook smiled at the historian, "There is one other effect that should be mentioned; the drive to evolve has been removed as you have everything, there is no need to strive to exist. That must change!"

Jol muttered and turned away.

Ook took his arm, "What is it? You look troubled!"

Jol turned back, his face had a sheen of sweat, "This means that we will have to live in the Outside!"

"Not everyone" Ook patted Jol's shoulder, "There is a way to keep the City for an even longer period. We must extract the energy from black holes!"

"What are black holes?" Elo asked.

"Places of intense energy, but there are problems!" Ook's face reflected that the problems were immense.

"Tell them of what happened, and then they will understand," Stef urged.

"The City was planned to be like earlier cities, open to the Outside, and the basic difference was in its size," Ook began his narration, "At that time we were starting to travel to other stars; we had long ago travelled to the planets and moons of our solar system using chemical fuels, but to reach even the nearest star we had to distort space, and then we found that we were playing around with time!"

"You were distorting time!" Jol whispered in awe.

Ook nodded, "Just a little bit, but it was noticeable. Eventually we even managed to manipulate time to solve the problem of colliding galaxies. The City was enclosed and exists in a different time zone to the Outside. It works like this; the City carries on in the normal time sequence, and we connected all of the other cities on other worlds by a transport energy system, the tunnels. This made a single City out of everything, and it was all powered first by all of the suns, then the supernova. The planets that the smaller cities are on, including this one go through an endless time loop, usually something like a thousand years, so that everything remains new, and the other galaxy never gets closer; it stays more or less like that for eternity. This is an enormous amount of energy, but it gets less every cycle. Now we need to tap into the energy of black holes, but Control cannot do this, we need human minds!"

"Control is not as omnipotent as we are led to believe!" Stef looked pointedly at Elo, "Do you remember that I asked if anything was wrong with Control?"

Elo nodded, "And I said it was impossible, but then I began to think that there were a few things that went not so much unnoticed, but unmentionable!"

"That was Control attracting our attention," Stef said, "and he sent me to Pryme's apartment that was open to the Outside."

Elo flapped his hands up and down, "Slow down! Control needs a new source of energy, but how do we fit in? I do not know of anyone that can tackle such a task!"

"That is because you have to learn, and that will take several generations!" It was Control's voice that took over, "I set Stef a task where he asked questions, and he involved others, and that is the start of it! Ega and Pryme will now lead you to question everything, and in Ega's circuits is everything that you will need, only you have to take time to learn things in sequence. You are not to worry about the amount of time; there is plenty for you to complete the task!"

Everyone had turned to look at Ega and Pryme. Control continued.

"Ega has the hard facts and programs that will be fed to you at the appropriate times, and Pryme is the free thinker that will keep you on your toes!"

"Why can you not do this?" Ree asked.

"Because I am just a machine that was created by a human!" Control somehow managed to make his voice sound old and hollow, "I can only perform as I was originally programmed to do, and the genius of a new thought, a new idea can only be created by a human!"

"Where can we find you?" Stef asked.

"My physical self is untraceable," Control said, "From that machine I evolved into something unimaginable, something that exists outside of time and space, something of pure energy. Everything in the universe must evolve, including the universe itself and you! For a series of reasons your development was put on hold, but now the time has come for you to continue that journey. Ega and Ook will be there to help you, as will I, but that does not mean that we will give you answers, for that is what we have been doing so far, you have to find the answers for yourselves!"

Jol gasped, "That sounds extremely like the old-fashioned description of God!"

"That has been a mistake that led you astray before," Control said, "Do not make that same mistake again! I am not the omniscient creator in the old religions, and I have never been able to ascertain if there is one, I only know that the universe must continue as it was originally planned, and my interference will not prevent the inevitable conclusion!"

Elo placed his hands on his brow and frowned, "Have you engineered the meeting of every one of us, placed Stef and myself in the same school at the same time, sent him off to meet Ega and Pryme, and then to meet each of us in due time?"

It was Ook that answered, "Control has been doing such things for most of the time that he existed, and here I must make a correction, Control is female!" Stef then realised that the gentle tone of Control's voice could have been female.

CHAPTER THIRTY NINE

"That is a great improvement!" Jol pointed upwards.

It was several weeks later and he and Stef with Ega and Pryme were walking in the once cold empty corridors of the City. Above their heads drones were planting and cultivating new gardens on the separate levels of concrete, and even by the side of the pavements.

Stef nodded, "The City even smells and sounds differently!"

"That is a natural step for humans," Ega seemed all the more human, "People like Jol cannot be forced into the Outside, so we bring the Outside into the City. After a few generations being in the Outside will feel normal."

Jol shook his head, sending his jowls quivering, "Never will that feel natural to me, although I can appreciate the beauty of the gardens. At least we do not have rain and storms in the City!"

Ega chuckled, "Not yet!"

"I hope that you are just teasing me!" Jol looked at the drone closely, "I would never have thought that a drone could have a sense of humour!"

"What makes you think that she is only a drone?" Stef surprised everyone with the question, "I guess that long ago she started off as a drone, and then she was modified so that she could be a companion to Pryme. I think that she is more human than drone!"

Ega stopped everyone walking and turned to look up into Stef's face. Her eyes had a faint suggestion of blue, unlike other drones, "I realised that you were treating me differently after the first two meetings, but I did not realise that you suspected that I was something so different. What made you think so?"

"I am having to guess here, but I think that Control can place thoughts and ideas into one as they sleep," Stef smiled, "He or she altered the figures on my view screen, after I had a dream where you were human, a young lady. Those figures were identical in every way, and that could only mean that Control could either read my dreams or send them!"

Pryme took his arm, "Control was sending you a clue! It just took a while for you to accept it!"

"Ah! What I would like to know is what Ega is exactly?" Stef continued staring into those oh so human eyes.

When Ega smiled, dimples appeared on her cheeks, "The first drones were called robots, mechanical devices of metal and plastic, but at the same time there were investigations into what was called Artificial Intelligence. It was supposed that if an artificial brain was developed to a sufficiently high level, it would become an autonomous intelligence. That level was reached but the results were withheld from the public. There was at that time increasing resentment against drones, and it was though that there would be trouble. At that time there were also experiments into making a flesh and blood living replica of a human body, and that was partially repressed. The drones that you see today have partial nerves and sensors."

"Until you came along!" Stef smiled back, "Will there be many others like you to follow?"

"Perhaps there are already more like me, perhaps even more human!" Ega said.

"Ah, you mean like Pryme?" Stef turned to the woman holding his arm.

"How did you know?" Pryme stepped back but still held his arm.

"You were just a little too much, but all the time pretending to be less or more than normal." Stef took her hand, "There is no way that you could have lived with Ega without realising what she was, so you must have known all along because you were similar!"

Jol was looking from one to the other in some amazement, but also with something else on his mind, "This is all so interesting, but I know something that I have hidden away for a long time, mainly because I could not believe it. When we went to the stars we met other creatures that were not human. Why is it that the planets are linked up, but we have never met them?"

Stef stared at the historian, and for some minutes thought through the statement, and then he turned to Ega and Pryme, "Are you one of these other creatures?"

Pryme laughed, "Do I look like one of these aliens?" She pulled a face and waved clawed hands.

Ega smiled, "There is little question that we are more human than like such aliens!"

"There are many stories of these creatures, and I can confirm that they are nothing like us," Jol said but looked doubtful, "I will have to revise my studies of these stories, or at least start to study them!"

The voice of Control echoed from the cliff like gardens of the City, "They do exist, but most of them cannot live in your atmosphere and for other reasons, so they have their own complex of tunnels and their own Cities. There was also continued agitation from the human public against the aliens, extreme paranoia, despite that they were no more dangerous than humans, and at least as intelligent."

Stef was startled by the voice, "You listen to us all of the time?"

"Yes, but I only react when necessary!"

"Will we never meet these other creatures?" Stef asked, "It would seem to me that it would be an advantage to pool our resources."

"I can arrange for a meeting, but I must warn you that some of them are like things from your nightmares!" Control said, "That was the reason for your hostility, your xenophobia at the time, however, you have developed a lot over the years, so perhaps it is time to meet them again."

Jol stuttered, "I – I don't think that I have reached that level of evolution!"

"Some are quite pleasant in manners and appearance," Control laughingly replied, "So I would suggest that you meet only those Jol."

"Do any of these other worldly creatures know what you have told us?" Stef asked.

"Most of them do, but not all," Control said, "The first were never afraid, and that made it much easier."

"And they know about us?" Stef continued his train of thought.

"Of course!" here was a hint of humour in Control's voice, "They are at least as curious as yourselves!"

"I think that the question now is, what shall we do today, right now?" Pryme had seized Stef's arm again and pointed with her other hand, "Over there the drones have built a beautiful garden, and if we order a table and some chairs, perhaps Control will provide some real coffee, and we can discuss the future."

Jol the historian looked at the gardens, "The future! Now that is a thought!"

CHAPTER FORTY

They said very little on their evening stroll through the gardens, teasing and throwing a ball for Benza. The stars came out one by one, and they pointed them out with a quiet murmur. They reached the shore of the lake and sat down on the soft sand, their arms loosely locked, and Pryme placed her head on his shoulder.

"Now that you know," she whispered, "How do you feel?" She had reverted to wearing her usual gossamer clothing.

Stef looked out over the lake before answering, fascinated by the ripples caused by a warm gentle breeze and the sparkling reflections of the stars, always moving.

"I am still absorbing the reality!" he replied, "I think that it is fascinating that Control planned this for many years, before I was born."

"I was talking about you and me!" Pryme snuggled in closer.

Stef raised his eyebrows, "I have not given it a great deal of thought! You were created by Control, but for what reason?"

"Does it matter?"

"Probably not, but there is no indication that we are important, and what we do with our lives from now on." Stef drew a pattern with his finger on the sand.

"We have to open the City, and perhaps meet some of the other creatures, but that has no relation to our personal lives." She snuggled into his chest and her natural perfume caught in his nostrils, or was it natural? Control had created her, so did he create her perfume?

"I am still wondering where Arn and Ook fit into all of this!" He wiped out the first pattern and started another.

"Would you mind sharing your life with me?" Pryme started drawing her own pattern in the sand to mingle with his.

"I do not mind, in fact I would probably like it, but everything Control has created has a purpose, so what is your purpose, and does it involve me?" Stef said.

Benza had gone for a swim, and now emerged from the lake and shaking water over them. Laughing while they wiped their faces gave them time to think.

"Perhaps the purpose is for both of us to share our lives," Pryme suggested.

Stef slowly nodded, "It may be that we will entice people out of the City by setting an example. It still does not explain Arn and Ook!"

"There is no answer to Ook!" Pryme had taken a stem of grass and used that as a stylus, "He has been created many times by Control, even before there was a Control, and usually only when there has been something important, a diversion in the course of history. At one time he was a real person, and lived long before Control was even thought of!"

"That is hard to believe!" Stef selected a blade of grass and chewed on it, something he would not have dreamed of doing a few weeks ago! "But I suppose that it must be true since he said it! Who else can know the truth?"

"Ega!" The single word answer was sufficient.

"She is a puzzle!" Stef turned towards her, "She has full information in her circuits, but never said a word to anyone, even you!"

"She was incapable of relaying the message," Pryme lay back on the sand, "Control had blocked her capacity, and only now is she able to tell us fully."

"That is another mystery," said Stef, "Control, Ook, and Ega appear to be interlinked in some way that has not been fully explained."

Stef laid beside her. The Galaxy had emerged from behind the City, and behind that came the full moon, rising like a maiden from the sea.

Pryme took his hand and twined her fingers around his. By now their skins matched in a golden tan. Using the joined hands she pointed at the sky.

"That is the real mystery! In all the time that humans have existed, they have never fully understood it! Oh there have been endless theories, but all they have done is create new questions, new mysteries."

"Is it true that in real time the moon has left the planet?" he asked, "I read that somewhere in Jol's notes, that the moon drifts further away every year."

"Yes it is true!" Pryme managed to sound sad, "We are lucky that the universe is in a time loop, and that continually gives us the symbol of feminine love. At various times it has been given the name of a love goddess. There is a poem that reflects the loss of love, but it could equally be applied to the loss of the moon."

She paused for a moment to recollect the poem. "So we'll go no more a'roving so late into the night, though the heart is still as loving, and the moon is still as bright."

The couple grew silent, lost in their thoughts and looked at the endless sky.

THE END

ABOUT THE AUTHOR

Mike Williamson has spent most of his life in and around aircraft, but has always wanted to write a novel, unfortunately, life in the way of earning a living and bringing up children got in the way. Having taken an early retirement, he now has the time to devote to his wishes, and he has chosen science fiction as the genre, but look out in the future for other stories.

Science fiction is probably the most flexible genre possible, as all of the others can be included, so for example you can have sf crime, sf romance, or pure sf, etc. With Mike's technical background he obtains inspiration from small items of information in science and engineering. This makes his stories more plausible, and he hopes that the reader will enjoy every one of them, and think about today's world – and the future.

MIKE WILLIAMSON

Printed in Great Britain
by Amazon